Whispering Brook Farm

Carrie Bender

Herald
Press

Scottdale, Pennsylvania
Waterloo, Ontario

Library of Congress Cataloging-in-Publication Data
Bender, Carrie, date.
    Whispering Brook Farm / Carrie Bender.
        p. cm.
    Summary: Depicts the life of the Petersheims, a large,
close-knit Amish family living on a farm in Lancaster
County, Pennsylvania.
    ISBN 0-8361-9011-4
    [1. Amish—Fiction. 2. Farm life—Fiction. 3. Family life
—Fiction.] I. Title.
PZ7.B43136Wh 1995
[Fic]—dc20   94-39706

The paper used in this publication is recycled and meets the
minimum requirements of American National Standard for
Information Sciences—Permanence of Paper for Printed Library
Materials, ANSI Z39.48-1984.

WHISPERING BROOK FARM
Copyright © 1995 by Herald Press, Scottdale, Pa. 15683
        Published simultaneously in Canada by Herald Press,
        Waterloo, Ont. N2L 6H7. All rights reserved
Library of Congress Catalog Card Number: 94-39706
International Standard Book Number: 0-8361-9011-4
Printed in the United States of America
Book design by Paula Johnson
Cover art and illustrations by Joy Dunn Keenan

05 04 03 02 01 00 10 9 8 7 6 5
Over 26,500 copies in print

To order or request information, please call
1-800-759-4447 (individuals); 1-800-245-7894 (trade).
Website: www.mph.org

Whispering Brook Farm

Books by Carrie Bender

Miriam's Journal Series
A Fruitful Vine
A Winding Path
A Joyous Heart
A Treasured Friendship
A Golden Sunbeam
Miriam's Cookbook

Whispering Brook Series
Whispering Brook Farm
Summerville Days
Chestnut Ridge Acres
Hemlock Hill Hideaway

Dora's Diary Series
Birch Hollow Schoolmarm
Lilac Blossom Time

*To my
beloved family*

Scripture is based on *King James Version of the Holy Bible*, adapted toward current English usage. Lines from "Ringe Recht . . ." are from *Church and Sunday School Hymnal* (MPH/Herald Press, 1902), Deutscher Anhang, no. 10. "How Great Thou Art" is available in *The Mennonite Hymnal* (Herald Press, 1969), no. 535. "Home, Sweet Home" is quoted from John Howard Payne; "Ask me no questions" from Oliver Goldsmith; "God's in his heaven" from Robert Browning; "Life is real! . . . Dust thou art" from Henry Wadsworth Longfellow; "All this and heaven too" from Matthew Henry; and "All is well that ends well" from John Heywood. The baptismal service is based on Donald B. Kraybill, *The Riddle of Amish Culture* (Baltimore: Johns Hopkins, 1989) and otherwise verified.

Note

This story is fiction,
but true to Amish life.
Any resemblance to persons living
or dead is coincidental.

Contents

1

The Secret Perch

SATURDAY evening on the Petersheim farm: The hurry and work of the day was over, and sweet peace settled over the picturesque countryside. The white lilac bush beside the washhouse door gave a delicate fragrance to the evening air. In the barnyard, two little brown Jersey calves with soft, sweet eyes stood looking over the fence at the playful antics of Snowball and Calico, two of the farm's kittens.

The old apple orchard in back of the barn rang with the merry laughter of Omar, Steven, and Henry.

They were playing ball tag, under trees that great-grandfather Petersheim had planted years ago.

The barking of Lassie, their tawny-and-white collie dog, mingled with their shouts as she romped with them. In the pasture field, *Daed* (Dad) was checking a fence for necessary repairs next week.

The barn door opened, and a whistling Joe emerged, leading Chief, his new standardbred horse, harnessed and ready to be hitched to the buggy. Sixteen-year-old Joe was just beginning his *rumschpringe* years (going out with the youths). To-morrow night would be his first at the young people's singing. Tonight, he and his sister Mary were invited to a volleyball game at a friend's house.

Eighteen-year-old Mary came demurely out of the house, dressed up and ready to go with Joe. She chatted briefly with grandma and grandpa, who were sitting on rockers on their porch. Musical joy rang out as she called good-bye; Mary was a great one for laughter. She was the picture of wholesomeness, from her white prayer covering and neatly combed hair down to her polished shoes.

Chief was a spirited horse. With a lunge and a flurry of gravel, they were off.

As the youths passed, *Mamm* (Mom) and three-year-old Susie waved to them from the garden. They were strolling along the path, among rows of peas, potatoes, lettuce, and other early vegetables. From a nearby tree, a robin flung its cheery notes into the sweet evening air.

High in the maple tree beside the barn, nine-year-old Nancy swayed, watching and listening to the evening activity. No one had discovered her secret hiding place yet. To get to it, she had to climb up into the haymow in the barn, then out the barn window onto a limb. She had found a comfortable seat where three branches grew out from the main trunk. None of the limbs were low enough to be reached from the ground, and this was the only reason the boys hadn't discovered her hiding place.

From her lofty perch, Nancy could see all the dells, slopes, and fields of the entire farm. She could see the fir grove with its dark shadows, the friendly, beloved old orchard, and the row of Lombardy poplars to the east. She treasured every inch of the farm, but best of all was the misty, buttercup-filled meadow, through which Whispering Brook flowed. Nancy delighted in naming trees, paths, and brooks because she loved them so dearly.

There was a cozy, shady nook where the brook flowed around a curve and over smooth stones. There Nancy liked to sit and dream, soaking up the tranquillity and beauty surrounding her. The water made a gentle, whispering sound as it flowed. At first Nancy thought it was only the wind rustling through the trees. But one day she had heard the whispering when not even the tiniest breeze was stirring, so she knew it was the stream. From that day on, she called it Whispering Brook.

When Nancy wanted to choose a name for their

home, no other name pleased her as well as Whispering Brook Farm. However, she told no one else about the name. Only *englisch* (non-Amish) people named their farms, and she was sure her dad would not approve.

Over her head, a white board was wedged securely between the trunk and two side-by-side branches. Nancy reached up and pulled down her sign to admire it. In neat black letters, she had painted on it WHISPERING BROOK FARM. How she wished she dared nail it to the side of the barn. Then everyone driving in would know that this is Whispering Brook Farm. With a sigh, Nancy put the board back on its tree forks.

Twilight was creeping over the farm, and peaceful evening sounds floated to her. Jeremiah, the big bossy rooster, and his biddies had flown to their roosts for the night and were cackling softly to each other. A mockingbird sang a few notes, then quieted down for the night. In the sky, an evening star twinkled at Nancy, and through the branches of the tree she could see the silvery moon. A light went on in the grandparents' kitchen, and a moment later a light burned in their own kitchen as well.

Reluctantly Nancy left her perch and climbed in through the barn window. The sweet scent of hay from the mow greeted her, and a pigeon cooed sleepily from the rafters. There was a flash of white and grey, as Tabby, the mother cat, vanished behind a stack of hay bales. "Tomorrow I'll find her nest of

kittens," Nancy told herself. By now they must be several weeks old. In the stable below, the horses whinnied to her as she passed, and the cows contentedly chewed their cud.

Outside the barn, Nancy stood looking at the house. How dear it was, and the people in it! She always loved to stand outside after dark and look at its glowing windows. It was such a comfortable, friendly house, built of brown sandstone, with high ceilings and wide window seats in each room. A curved walk led from the veranda, under the rose arbor, past the windmill, then on out toward the barn.

The boys and Lassie came trooping in from the orchard. "Where have you been?" cried Henry, next younger than Nancy. "We needed you to make our teams even."

"Probably sitting under a tree or beside the brook somewhere, dreaming of fairies and elves and moonbeams," teased Steven. He was a year older than Nancy and took a dim view of such things. Fourteen-year-old Omar was the only one who shared her love for dreams and fancies.

The kitchen door opened. "Come, children, it's time to take your baths," Mamm called from the porch. There was a chorus of groans from the boys. Saturday night was bath time.

"*Mamm* (Mom), may I take my bath at *Mammi's* (Grandma's) house again?" Nancy asked eagerly. She loved her parents dearly, but still there was something special about going to Mammi and

Daadi's (Grandpa's) end of the house. Somehow her grandma always understood exactly how Nancy felt. There was a merry twinkle in her eyes behind her gold-rimmed glasses, and her round face was framed by a halo of silvery white hair. Grandpa, too, was an understanding old soul and could be depended upon to take Nancy's side.

"Ask her if she doesn't mind," Mamm replied. "And don't forget to take your nightgown and housecoat along over."

The grandparents' kitchen was a cheery place. Geraniums bloomed at the windowsills, the black gas stove sparkled and shone, the walls and ceiling were painted with high-gloss white paint, and on the dry sink stood the familiar blue-and-white washbowl and pitcher set—the very one that Daadi had bought for Mammi when she was a bride.

After her bath, Nancy sat at the kitchen table across from where Daadi sat reading the big German Bible. Mammi poured her a glass of milk from the old-fashioned brown ceramic pitcher and set out a plate of oatmeal raisin cookies.

The Petersheim grandparents loved all the children of their son, Levi, but they had extra warm feelings in their hearts for Nancy, because she loved and needed them so much. Since childhood, she had come to them with her little hurts and fears and questions, and they had soothed her and answered her questions the best they could.

"Did you ever hear of an Amish farm with a

name, Daadi?" Nancy bent forward, eagerly awaiting his answer.

Daadi chuckled. "It seems to me I did. Wasn't there once one named Whispering Brook Farm?" His eyes twinkled at Nancy.

Nancy's eyes grew large. "Did you climb my tree?"

Grandpa threw back his head and laughed heartily. "No, a little bird saw it and came and told me."

"Now, Daadi, you can just stop your teasing," scolded Mammi. "Next she'll take you seriously. He peeped into the shop when you were painting your sign, Nancy."

"Did you think it was dumb?" Nancy asked, looking hopeful.

"No indeed! I thought it was clever. And if you want me to, I'll put up your sign for you, right up on the middle of the barn for all to see."

"Will you really, Daadi? But what will Daed (Dad) say?" Nancy was breathless with excitement.

"He won't say anything if I put it up. I'm still boss of this farm," Daadi boasted.

"Oh, thank you, thank you!" Nancy jumped up and patted his stooped shoulder. "You're the bestest Daadi in the world."

"My, my, it's way past your bedtime," Mammi cried. "Off to bed with you."

Nancy snuggled happily under the covers. *Remembering to say your prayers is easy when you're happy,* she thought. She prayed for everyone living on Whispering Brook Farm, and for all the animals, too. Then she fell asleep, dreaming happy dreams.

2

Courtin' Time

THE house was astir with excitement on Sunday evening a week later. The whole family had been to church at Cousin Elam's, in a neighboring district. They had opened folding doors between rooms, carried backless benches in from the church's bench wagon, and set them in neat rows. On Saturday, to make room for the benches, some of Elam's furniture had been stored in the bench wagon. On Sunday morning, some of the beds were taken apart and set aside. Then the congregation crowded in.

After the singing of the slow tunes, the preacher delivered his sermon from the doorway between the living room (with men and boys) and the huge farm kitchen (with women, girls, and small children). When church was over, tables were set up, and the women served a simple meal of rolls, spreads, smearcase (cottage cheese), pickles, and *Schnitzboi* (dried-apple pies).

When the family had all come home again, Joe let the cat out of the bag and told the thrilling news. Mary was having a beau take her out tonight! Nancy hugged herself. She could hardly wait until 7:00! There would be no singing or other gathering tonight, so he would come directly to Mary's home. Nancy planned to climb to her tree hideaway and watch him drive in, tie his horse, and walk to the parlor door.

"Who's the lucky fellow?" Dad asked at the supper table.

Mary blushed a deep shade of pink.

"One of Henner Crist's boys," Joe kidded, with a mischievous look at Mary.

"Joe!" Mary cried, aghast. "You stop lying!"

Crist was the son of Henner Glick, and his boys were wild and rough. The two oldest were regularly seen tearing through the neighborhood, recklessly and irresponsibly, in their new red Porsche. They were not church members.

"Okay, okay, I'll stop teasing," relented Joe. "It's one of Steph's Dan's Mose's boys."

"So?" Dad responded. "That's a fine family. What's his name?"

"Jacob."

"What's his last name?" piped up Nancy.

"Yoder," Mom replied.

"Oh, so it's Jeckie Yedder!" Henry quipped. Everyone laughed. The whole family was having fun at Mary's expense.

Mary took the ribbing in good humor, but soon she got up from the table, not able to eat a bite of supper. There were butterflies in her stomach. She went out and sat on the porch swing. Mary thought the house looked a bit weatherbeaten, and the barn was soon due for a coat of paint. Mose Yoder's farm was shipshape. Would Jacob think their place was shabby? She hoped not.

The purple martins chirped and warbled as they flitted around their blue-and-white, three-story martin house. Mary took a deep breath. The air was fresh and cool, after an afternoon shower. Two robins were hopping in the yard, cocking their heads, and listening for worms. Mary decided to take a walk in the orchard. Maybe that would calm her nervousness.

There was a queer little ache in her heart—not a stab of unhappiness, but an ache nevertheless. Having her first date! If they both wanted to go on seeing each other, in a few years she would be getting married.

How could she bear to think of leaving this place

and her dear family? It all seemed so indescribably beautiful tonight. The dear trees in the fir wood, the fields and the meadow and the brook, and all the other familiar scenes where she loved to roam. But now it was time to go back to the house. Before long it would be 7:00.

Mom came in from the milking. Seven o'clock came and went, but there was no courtin' buggy in sight yet. Mary was pacing back and forth in the kitchen. She went to the mirror to brush back some imaginary stray hairs, then to the east window, then over to the one facing west.

"Sit down and try to relax," Mom soothed her. "Maybe he wanted to make sure he's not too early—and miscalculated a little."

"*Mamm* (Mom), where's Nancy?" Mary asked impatiently. "She could go up to the fir grove and see if he's coming up the Covered Bridge Road."

"I'll go," Susie offered eagerly. She trotted out the door.

The clock showed 7:45. Joe came in, having finished the chores. "What!" he exclaimed. "I never thought Jacob would be a slacker. Maybe it was all a big joke."

"Well, you sure are Job's comforter!" Mary retorted. "You're welcome to go back outside!"

"Oh, I'm sorry," Joe said meekly, seeing how upset Mary was. "It's not that late yet. Maybe his horse got lame on the way here."

Susie came in, banging the screen door. "I

23

looked and looked, but I couldn't see any Jeckie." She was so disappointed that Mary had to laugh in spite of herself.

Up in the maple tree, Nancy sat on her perch, waiting and waiting. "It must be about bedtime," she muttered darkly. "I wonder what's keeping him. I think I'll go hunt for that nest of kittens for awhile."

Finally at 8:30, Jacob came, in a shiny new buggy with a prancing black horse hitched to it. To tie his horse, he drove to a hitching ring under Nancy's maple tree.

"He's here, he's here!" shouted Susie. Mary's butterflies began to flutter in earnest.

"He's tying his horse," Susie reported. "Look, Mary, I'm glad he doesn't have a beard!"

"Of course not," Mary responded. "You know, boys don't have beards until they get married."

Meanwhile, Nancy had found the nest of kittens and decided to go to the house to find out what was going on. She opened the barn door and gasped in surprise. There stood Jacob, tying his horse. Nancy thought she would turn around and go back into the barn, but then Jacob smiled and said, "Hello. I'm rather late. Is Mary still waiting for me?"

"Ah, er—er—I think so," Nancy stammered. "What happened?"

"Some guys in a car pelted me with rotten *Grummbeere* (potatoes). I had to turn around and go home to clean up and change clothes. What a mess!"

"How awful!" For a bit, Nancy forgot her shyness. "Do you know the guys?"

"No, it was just some young boys out looking for mischief. Someone had cleaned out their potato bin and dumped them near the road. Say, can you tell me which is the parlor door? Is it the first or the second door on the front porch?"

"The second," Nancy informed him. "The first is grandpa's sitting-room door."

"Thanks a lot!" He gave her a smile.

He's really good-looking, Nancy thought as she watched him walk to the porch. *And nice and friendly, too.*

The boys had given up waiting for Jacob and gone for a walk in the meadow. Now they came trooping back, wanting to hear all about Jacob. Nancy was bursting with importance: she was the first one to talk with Jacob and could tell them the story, that he had been pelted with rotten potatoes. They sat in a circle under the clump of birch trees, discussing Jacob and Mary.

Dusk was settling over the fields and meadow. It was that tender time of day when twilight pulls its curtain down and pins it with a star. Calico and Snowball were romping among the children, and the birch leaves were rustling silkily overhead.

"I heard Daed say to Mamm tonight, while we were milking, that he thinks Jacob and Mary would make a good match," Omar told them.

"Sshh!" whispered Steven. "Next they'll hear

you. There they are, going out the lane for a walk." They watched until the couple was swallowed up by the misty twilight.

"I hope they do marry," Henry commented. "Having a wedding would be fun, with lots of good food!"

"Just look at that!" Nancy suddenly exclaimed, pointing across the field. "The Cooper place is all lit up. Do you think it's a robbery?"

The Cooper place was an old stone house, built in the 1700s, that had stood empty for the last ten years. Rumor had it that George Washington had once spent the night there, but no one knew whether or not that was really true. It was the oldest building in the area.

"Maybe a family moved in," Henry suggested. "If they were thieves, they wouldn't light up so many rooms. Besides, what would there be to steal in an empty house?"

Before long, the kitchen door opened, and Daed called them to bed.

Tomorrow Daadi will put up my WHISPERING BROOK FARM sign, Nancy thought happily as she prepared for bed. *I wonder what Jacob will think of it?*

3

Strawberries

It was strawberry time at Whispering Brook Farm. The Petersheims had an acre, so everybody had to help pick berries. Daed paid ten cents for each quart they picked. Usually they didn't get paid for work they did, but picking strawberries was different.

"My, it's chilly this morning," Steven complained, shivering. He and Nancy were picking side by side. "I feel like going for gloves."

"Just wait till the sun gets higher. Then you'll soon wish for some of this coolness," warned

Nancy. "I can pick faster when it's cool, and I'd like to make ten dollars today. I'm saving to buy a new scooter, one all my own."

"Henry and I are putting our money together to buy a new saddle. I wish I could pick as fast as Mary. She made twenty dollars yesterday."

Henry came out to the field with a stack of quart boxes. "Guess what Daadi is doing," he chattered excitedly. "He's up on a ladder, putting a sign on the barn that says WHISPERING BROOK FARM. When Daed saw it, he said he wonders if Daadi is getting into his second childhood."

"Is that all he said?" Nancy asked eagerly. "Was he disgusted?" But Henry had already run off to tell the others.

Steven laughed. "I can tell that you had something to do with it. It was your idea, wasn't it?"

Nancy pretended she hadn't heard. "Ask me no questions, and I'll tell you no lies," she sang out.

Steven abruptly changed the subject. "Say, Nancy, what do you think is the matter with Mamm? Other years she always helped pick strawberries, and this year she's not helping at all. I wonder if she's getting lazy.

"And did you notice how much *Millich* (milk) she drinks at the table? With every meal, she fills her glass with *Millich* instead of water. Then on Sunday, she didn't go along to church, even though she wasn't sick. Do you think she's getting a little funny in the head?"

"Steven Petersheim!" Nancy rebuked him. Her brown eyes flashed fiercely. "You can stop talking like that! Mamm can drink a gallon of milk every day if she wants to. There's nothing wrong with her. She's not lazy either. Mamm's busy canning strawberries while we pick, and she's already put up more than a hundred quarts."

"Okay, okay, I take it back," Steven muttered. "Just don't blow your top like that. It doesn't fit you."

Susie came out from the house just then. Her eyes sparkled. "I've got a secret!" she crowed. "I'm not allowed to tell you. But it's something that tastes good. We're having it for dinner."

"Homemade strawberry ice cream!" Steven yelled. "Whoopee!"

Susie looked crestfallen. "You weren't supposed to guess." A tear slid down over her cheek. "Mary will think I told you."

"Cheer up, Sister," Steven comforted her. "We won't let on that we figured it out. I'm glad I do know, because it's something to look forward to. Then maybe I can stand to pick berries all morning."

"That's right," Nancy added. "Now when my back aches, I'll just think of delicious ice cream, and I won't mind it as much."

"Mary's going to ask you to help crank the freezer yet, when you come in." Susie trotted off to where Joe and Omar were picking.

When the dinner bell rang, Nancy and Steven hurried in. Steven rushed to finish cranking the freezer of ice cream, and Nancy ran over to see the sign on the barn.

There it was, looking even better than she thought it would. For all to see, it announced WHISPERING BROOK FARM. Nancy's heart felt satisfied at the sight of it.

Grandma and Grandpa were having dinner with them today. When Nancy went into the pantry for a loaf of homemade bread, she saw a large, white, splendidly iced cake, with "Happy Birthday, Daed" on it. So that was behind the celebration! She had forgotten all about today being Daed's birthday.

Mammi and Daadi were seated at the head of the table, and they all bowed their heads to ask a silent blessing on the food. Mamm passed the platter of fried chicken and a dish heaped high with fluffy mashed potatoes. The main topic of the conversation was the sign on the barn.

"Whose idea was it, anyway?" Joe wanted to know.

Grandpa caught Nancy's eye and winked broadly. Nancy blushed. She knew that Daadi wouldn't give away her secret.

"What will . . . uh . . . the neighbors think?" Mary wondered. She caught herself just in time to keep from saying, *What will Jacob think?*

"Since when does what the neighbors think determine what we do?" Daadi asked mildly.

When Mary carried in the cake and handed it to her dad, the sign was completely forgotten. Everyone joined in singing, "Happy Birthday to You."

Dad beamed his appreciation. "Thanks to every one of you." He cut the cake into generous pieces. "It's nice to be remembered."

Mom dished out the ice cream.

"I want to lick the dasher," Susie volunteered. "It's my turn."

Nancy looked at each person around the table as she slowly ate her ice cream, savoring each bite. *It's so nice to have the family all together like this,* she thought. *I wish it could always stay like this, and no one would ever leave home.*

Her gaze rested on her mom. *She really is pretty,* Nancy thought. *Her cheeks are pink, and she has smiling eyes.* Mamm was drinking a glass of milk. Suddenly Nancy remembered what Steven had said and felt vaguely troubled. Her mother had gained a lot of weight, and it was true that she drank a glass of milk at each meal and that she didn't help pick strawberries.

Nancy had scolded Steven severely for saying what he did, but now it began to bother her. She decided to ask Mammi about it sometime. Her grandmother always had an answer for her questions.

The meal was over, and the family bowed their heads to thank God for the food.

4

New Girl

JOE was late for the singing one Sunday evening. Since Mary had started going with Jacob, he had slipped into the habit of arriving just as the singing began.

Chief was a good road horse and needed no urging. As soon as he felt the reins slacken a bit, he picked up speed. Joe was satisfied with him. Chief was up-headed and could make good time, but Joe wished he'd stand a little better at the crossings. Sometimes it took all the muscles he had to keep the

standardbred from lunging out before the road was clear.

As Joe drove in the lane, familiar strains of music floated out the open windows on the summer evening air. Boys' and girls' voices blended in singing hymns. He tied his horse and felt a thrill of anticipation. So far, *Rumschpringe* had been great.

Elmer and Ben, two of his buddies, came out of the barn and joined him.

"It's about time," Ben chided. "We were about to go in without you." Together they walked toward the house.

"Say, Joe, are you about ready to ask a girl for a date tonight?" Elmer teased, poking an elbow into Joe's ribs. "You could have the pick of the crop."

"Nah. You go ahead and choose your *Aldi* (girl friend). I'm still treating them all alike. What's the big hurry?"

The boys found a few empty seats left in the kitchen and were soon singing with the rest. Joe glanced across the room. Who was that new girl standing beside Mary? He stared, fascinated. She was tall with wavy brown hair, and her eyes were bright and captivating. Somehow, compared to her, the other girls appeared a bit drab. She was laughing and talking to the girl on the other side of her.

"Psst, Joe, quit staring at the girls and help sing," Ben teased. "I thought you weren't interested in girls yet."

"Who's that new girl?" Joe whispered back, ignoring Ben's teasing. "I've never seen her before."

"It's Amelia Mast from Summerville, boarding at her aunt and uncle's place so she can be with the young folks here."

Joe forced himself to help sing, but somehow his eyes were drawn to Amelia again and again, just like a magnet. Once their eyes met, and a little smile played across her lips. Joe's heartbeat quickened. Was this what they called "love at first sight"?

Mary and Jacob prepared to leave as soon as the singing was over, as the couples usually did. Mary got her bonnet and shawl and stood at the front gate, waiting for Jacob to drive up. A few other girls stood waiting, too. Mary strained her eyes in the darkness and wondered, *Is this Jacob, and his horse, King, driving up now?* Mary had a secret fear that sometime she might get into the wrong buggy.

The driver reined the impatient horse to a stop in the darkness, then stepped out. *No, that isn't Jacob.* Another girl stepped forward and climbed in. The horse, angered at being stopped so soon after starting off, reared and pawed the air, then started off with a lunge; the buggy wheels whirled. Next to drive up was Jacob, and he stepped down with the reins while Mary climbed in.

Soon they were going out the lane at a brisk trot. "Well, at least King's behaving himself tonight," Mary observed with a laugh.

"I think he's still improving. He's young yet." Jacob tucked in the buggy spread—the night air was cool. "Say, who was the new girl at the singing, the one who was standing beside you?"

"So you noticed the *schee Meedel* (pretty girl), too?" Mary teased. "She's Amelia Mast of Summerville."

"*Schee?* Who said anything about *schee?* She's not half as *schee* as you are," Jacob was quick to reply.

Mary smiled at the compliment, but Jacob couldn't see her face as he continued. "Putting on airs and rolling her eyes around, that's what she does. But I noticed that your brother Joe was smitten with her."

"Oh, no! I hope not! I hope he won't pick a girl like that."

"He was watching her most of the evening, if that means anything." The ride home was only a few miles, and soon they were driving in the lane at Whispering Brook Farm.

"Looks like there's a car parked in the lane." Jacob peered through the darkness.

Mary caught her breath. *Oh, dear, not tonight of all nights,* she thought.

"Do you think it might be the *Geilsdokder* (horse doctor, vet)?" Jacob drove up to the tie ring.

"Uh . . . er . . . . no, I don't think so," Mary stammered. How could she tell him? Somehow it didn't seem proper to talk to one's boyfriend about having babies, and such women's things.

"Do you think maybe someone's sick, and it's

35

the doctor's car?" Jacob persisted.

"No, I don't think it's the doctor. Probably it's the midwife." Mary blushed in the darkness. "Maybe we'd better just sit out here in the buggy instead of going in."

"Oh!" Jacob was surprised. "You . . . you mean. . . ." He stopped in embarrassment.

Mary nodded.

"I didn't know. Do you think I should leave right away?"

"No, this is all right, unless you'd rather go," Mary assured him. "If you like, we could go for a walk."

The moon was nearly full, and the evening fluttered with dancing, inviting shadows as they walked out the lane. An owl hooted from a tree in the meadow. The air smelled delicious.

"Maybe we should go down to Nancy's brook and listen to it whispering," Jacob chuckled. "I'd like to know what a whispering brook says." On Wednesday evening he had seen the sign on the barn when he picked up Mary to go to a watermelon party, and she had explained to him how it got there.

"Nancy must be quite a character," Jacob surmised.

Mary laughed. It was an infectious, bubbling laugh that Jacob liked to hear. "Nancy has some funny, romantic ideas, but we all love her anyway. We'll go down to the brook sometime when the grass isn't so wet. There's a heavy dew tonight."

When they came back and were starting in the lane, they met the midwife's car leaving. Mary felt a twinge of excitement. "I'll run into the house for just a few minutes," she told Jacob.

He stood waiting by his horse. A moment later she returned, glowing. "I have a new little sister. Daed told me he's going to name her Lydia, after Mamm, if she agrees."

"That's nice," Jacob said huskily. "This will make you rather busy, won't it?"

"Yes, but I don't mind. Having a new baby sister is worth it."

"Okay, I'd better be going, then. I'll be seeing you on Sunday evening again."

Mary wasn't sure whether it was a statement or question, but she responded anyhow: "Yes."

She watched as Jacob drove out the lane, his buggy lights growing fainter and fainter before disappearing in the darkness. Then she skipped toward the house, joy radiating from her like fragrance from a rose. She could hardly wait to see the baby.

5

Englisch Neighbor

"OH, what a *schee* baby!" Nancy exclaimed rapturously on Monday morning. "Isn't she sweet?" Mary had brought little Lydia out of the bedroom for the whole family to see, and Nancy wanted to hold her first.

"Be careful! You might drop her," Joe teased. But Nancy held her as carefully as anyone would wish.

"Look at her crumpled little hands." Omar eyed the new bundle of humanity with wonder. "And it

looks like there are dimples in her cheek."

"Just like Mary's," Steven remarked.

Henry stroked the soft little cheeks with a finger. Dad brought Susie out of her crib. "Want to see your baby sister?" he asked.

"It's my baby," Susie cried, stretching out her arms for her.

Nancy laid the baby in her arms for a few moments, and Susie touched her cheek to the baby's face.

"Take the baby in to Mamm, now, and we'll eat breakfast," Dad told Nancy. He got down the big family Bible to read aloud a few verses, as he did every morning at the breakfast table.

In the bedroom, Nancy's eyes shone as she handed baby Lydia to her mother. "I'm so happy, Mamm!" she bubbled. "I feel like I should pinch myself to see if it's just a dream."

Mom smiled wearily. "You'll help Mary real well with the work now, I'm sure."

Nancy nodded. "But I'd rather hold the baby all the time."

After breakfast, Mary sorted the laundry in big piles on the washhouse floor. Early that morning she had filled the big iron kettle fitted into the top of the special warehouse furnace and built a fire underneath. Eventually the water was boiling hot, and she dipped pail after pail of the steaming hot water into the washing machine.

Now she was ready to fire up the gas engine. She pulled the starter cord until she was tired, but nothing happened. "Oh, this is so exasperating," she complained. "Just when I was in a hurry to get started."

Joe appeared in the washhouse doorway. "Need help?" he volunteered.

"You're just the one I wanted to see." Mary smiled. "Those muscles of yours would sure come in handy."

"Say, before I start this noisy thing, I'd like to talk with you a bit." Joe seemed half shy. "What did you think of Amelia Mast on Sunday evening?"

"You're not getting interested in her, are you?" Mary quickly asked.

"Why not?" Joe was half defensive. "She seems like a nice girl."

"But didn't you notice how she has her hair puffed up, and how small her prayer covering is, compared to the other girls'? She's not dressed in the *Ordnung* (church order, rules), either."

"No, I . . . uh . . . didn't think about it," Joe lamely admitted. "But don't you think she would change that as she gets older?"

"She might, but then again, she might not. If her attitude doesn't change . . . and she keeps on 'crowding the fence.' . . .Well, if you want my opinion, I'd advise you not to date her."

"But you're not being fair," Joe objected, almost

without realizing what he was saying. He yanked mightily on the starter rope.

Mary bit her lip. She sensed that Joe had his heart set on Amelia, and that he didn't want to hear any more of what she was saying. In a few seconds the engine roared to life, and Joe walked out the door. Mary called, "Thank you!" after him, above the noise of the engine, but Joe didn't even turn around.

Mary sighed. She knew she had offended him and was sorry about it, but what could she have said differently? Why was he so unreasonable, anyway? Her thoughts were troubled as she seized the wash stick to lift the steaming clothes out of the hot water. One by one she fed them through the wringer.

She took the basket of wet clothes out to the wash line, and soon the first load was flapping merrily in the breeze. Mary's heart cheered at the sight of it. *It sure is a pleasure to do the washing on a day like this,* she thought. The sky was blue and filled with little fluffy white clouds. The breeze would dry the wash in a hurry. How she hated it when the laundry didn't dry on the line, and she had to take it all in to the kitchen and hang everything on drying racks beside the stove. Those days she thought of how nice it would be to have an electric or gas clothes dryer.

Mary glanced out the lane. Who was that coming in, on a bicycle? Probably a girl from town. There were egg cartons on her carrier, so it must be an egg customer. Omar came out of the barn just as she drove up.

"Hi!" She smiled brightly. "I'm Jewell Vaneski. My parents and I just moved into that house across the fields from you." With her small shapely hand, she pointed to the Cooper place.

"Oh, you did?" Omar showed interest. "We saw a light there and were wondering about it." Most of the town girls wore shorts or slacks, but she was wearing a full-sleeved dress, covered with lace, ruffles, and shirring. It gave her a soft, feminine appearance. Her light brown hair was soft and fluffy around her face, making her appear almost angelic to Omar.

"I saw your EGGS FOR SALE sign at the end of the lane," she went on. "I'd like to buy two dozen." She handed the egg cartons to Omar, and he started for the chicken house.

"Oh please, may I come along?" Jewell begged. "I'd love to see the chickens. We moved all the way from California, and I'm dying of loneliness over there in that big house. Mom and Dad are away all the time, so it's only me and the servants. I'm tired of sitting in the house and watching TV."

"Don't you have any brothers and sisters?" Omar asked sympathetically.

"No, I'm an only child. Mom is a lawyer, and Dad is a stockbroker. How many brothers and sisters do you have?"

"Three brothers and three sisters—oops, I forgot. Yesterday a new baby arrived, so now it's four sisters."

Jewell's eyes opened wide. "Honest? A new baby?" She clasped her hands rapturously in front of her. "You people are so . . . so lucky. I wish I'd have been born Amish."

43

As Omar gathered the eggs, she crooned and fussed over the hens. Then she asked to be shown the other animals, too. On the way back to the yard, she spied the rose arbor, covered with the blooming red rambler roses.

"Ohhhh!" she breathed in ecstasy, walking over to the arbor. "This is too wonderful!" She raised a rose to her face and closed her eyes.

Omar felt almost embarrassed, but he looked at the roses with a new awe.

Jewell's face was almost worshipful. "If I bring my camera, will you snap a picture of me, standing under these heavenly roses? I'll show you how to do it. It's an Instamatic camera."

"I—I guess I could," Omar replied hesitantly.

"And then I'll take a picture of you standing under the roses, too," Jewell added. "I think we're likely about the same age."

"I'll be fifteen in September," Omar told her.

"You're kidding," exclaimed Jewell. "Which day?"

"The eighteenth."

"That's amazing. I'll be fifteen on September twenty-fifth. You're only one week older than I am. Why, we're almost twins!"

Omar's dad had gone a half mile down the road to make some calls from the phone shanty. Several Amish neighbors shared the use and the expense of it, for telephones are not allowed in Amish homes. They built a small wooden, outhouse-shaped building which served as a phone booth.

He had quite a few calls to make, and when he came back, a half hour later, he saw Omar still talking with that fancy *englisch* (non-Amish) girl who came for eggs. He would have to put a stop to that.

"Omar!" he called sharply. "It's time to get back to work."

"Oh, I'm so sorry." Jewell was contrite. "I'm keeping you from your work, and I must be leaving. I won't bother you any longer."

She pedaled swiftly down the lane. Omar was rather sorry to see her go. There was a winsomeness about her that appealed to him. She wasn't bold and brassy like some of the town girls who had come out to pick strawberries. He wished Daed hadn't spoken so sharply. Now she'd probably never come back.

6

Thunderstorm

"I wish it would rain," Steven sighed as he came into the house and flopped down on the settee. "It's so hot, dusty, and dry."

Mom came out of the bedroom with six-week-old baby Lydia.

"Would you hold her awhile for me?" she asked Steven. "The baby's so fussy. She minds this hot, sticky weather, too. Her back and neck are covered with heat rash. I'd like to make some peach dumplings for supper."

Joe came in for a glass of water. "I think it's going to storm," he observed. "There's an eerie calm. I don't like the looks of it."

Dad was calling from the barn: "C'mon boys! The south pasture hay field is fit for baling. Hurry! We'd like to get it in before it storms."

Steven laid the baby on the settee and ran out with Joe. This was more to his liking. Mary left the sewing machine, where she was making a white Sunday apron, and picked up the crying Lydia. "Where can that Nancy be?" she wondered. "She's always slipping off—whenever she has the chance."

"I think the heat is making everyone feel slack," Mom commented as she measured out three cups of flour. "She knows it's so much cooler out under the trees by the brook."

"The Whispering Brook, you mean," Mary corrected. She gently rocked Lydia until the baby fell asleep, then laid her in the crib. "There's something I think I should tell you, Mamm," Mary confided when she returned to the kitchen. "Maybe I should have talked to you about it sooner. It's about Joe. He's fallen for Amelia Mast—hook, line, and sinker."

"Amelia Mast?" Mom was puzzled. "You mean the girl from Summerville?"

"Yes, the one boarding at Cookie Dan's. She knows Joe's interested in her, and she's after him, too. I've tried to talk him out of it, but it's like talking to a brick wall. He has his mind made up."

"Isn't she a nice girl?" Then she quickly added,

"Joe is much too young to start going with any girl. Daed and I want all of our children to be church members before they choose a life partner."

"She's . . . well . . . she's rather flippant. She's *schee,* and she knows it, too. But she's not dressed in the *Ordnung.* She's not the kind of girl I'd have picked for Joe. Rather bold. She certainly doesn't have a meek and quiet spirit—far from it."

"Hmmmmm." Mom was thoughtful. "Daed and I will have to talk to him about it. To my way of thinking, sixteen is too young for dating, especially for the boys. They're still too immature to have the sense and good judgment they need. I wish we parents could all get together and do something about the age at which the young folks start to *rum-schpringe.*"

"Well, I hope you don't try anything like that," Mary objected. "You'd make yourself a lot of enemies in a short time. Remember, Jacob didn't start dating until he was twenty."

"Yes, and I respect him for it, too. He seems like a mature, dependable young man."

"My, look how dark the sky is getting. I hope they get that hay in before the storm gets here."

Just then Susie came out of the bedroom, looking tousle-headed after her nap. "I want a peach," she begged as she climbed on her Mother's lap.

Mom selected a juicy half from the bowl of peaches she had peeled for dumplings. There was a rumble of thunder in the west. A jagged fork of lightning zipped from cloud to cloud. Another rumble of thunder followed. Grandma and Grandpa came over from their kitchen.

"Where's Nancy?" Mammi seemed worried. "Isn't she afraid of *Dunner* (thunder) anymore?"

"Apparently not as much anymore, or she'd have been in awhile already." Mom replied, her mouth full of peach. "Here, help yourselves to some peaches." She passed the bowl to Mammi and Daadi.

"I wouldn't be surprised if we'd get some hail," Daadi predicted, peering out the west window. "See how pink the sky shines."

Down by Whispering Brook, Nancy sat watching the lightning zip from cloud to cloud. The thunder wasn't close yet, and it gave her a feeling of exhilaration to be out there. She lifted her skirts to her knees and danced and frolicked in the wind. On the hill, she could see Daed and the boys still out there, baling hay. As long as it was safe for them to be out, she would stay, too.

In the field, Dad kept urging the horses to go faster. They stacked bale after bale on the wagon. At least it was cooler now. Another two-pronged fork of lightning zapped from a cloud to the ground. There was a loud clap of thunder. Belle and Bo, the two big workhorses, pranced nervously. "Easy now," Dad tried to calm them. "Only a few more rows to go." He scanned the sky uneasily. It had a greenish hue now, an almost sinister glow.

"I think we'll quit now, even though we're not

finished," he shouted to the boys as he shut off the baler. "Drive to the barn." The wind whipped the words out of his mouth. There was a terrific crash of thunder. The horses were rushing toward the farm buildings.

"Run for the house," Dad called to the boys. He tied the horses in the stable and ran for the house, too. Nancy reached the porch just before he did. Her feeling of exhilaration at the rousing wind had now been replaced by healthy fear.

In the center of the kitchen, the family faced each other on a circle of chairs. "Stay away from the windows and the iron cookstove," Dad ordered. "If the *Wedderleech* (lightning) strikes the chimney, it could follow the pipe down to the stove."

There was a tense, electric feeling in the air. One sharp, terrifying crack of thunder followed the next. Susie began to whimper, and the younger boys sat wide-eyed, frightened.

"I wish it would start to rain," Mary moaned weakly. "Usually when it rains heavily, the *Wedderleech* and *Dunner* slacken off." A sharp crack and a boom drowned out her words.

Baby Lydia lay peacefully in her mother's arms, fast asleep and oblivious to the storm.

Suddenly the heavens opened and poured out a torrent of rain, which hammered against the windows.

"Listen!" Dad alerted them. There was a stinging sound against the west window, then another and another. It sounded like sleet.

In a moment, hail began to pelt against the house, and the wind rose to a shriek. There was a deafening roar as large hailstones, driven by the wind, rattled against the side of the house. A window cracked and broke, and soon the kitchen was filled with the sound of breaking glass.

"Shall we go to the cellar?" Mom asked anxiously.

"No," Daadi replied sharply. "We'll stay right here."

Mom wondered if he realized what he was saying or whether the confusion of the storm was getting to him. Yet soon the noise of the elements began to abate, and then it was over as suddenly as it had begun. The next thunderclap was fainter and further away. The rain stopped, and gradually the storm faded away in the distance.

"Might as well go and see what damage has been done," Dad decided. He got his hat and went outside, followed by the rest of the family.

"Oh, Daed, just look at the garden!" Mary cried in dismay. Where once neat rows of vegetables and flowers had been, now only shredded vines and leaves were spread on the ground.

"My *Beem* (trees)!" sobbed Nancy. She walked over to where a tall stately white birch had stood but now lay in a heap on the ground. Her maple tree by the barn was a pitiful sight, too, its leaves shredded, bedraggled, and limp.

51

Dad and the boys went to inspect the crops in the fields. The corn was stripped of its leaves; all that remained was the stalks. The neighbor's tobacco fields were completely demolished, with only stems left standing. "At least that tobacco won't defile anyone," Dad remarked thoughtfully."

Everywhere one looked, there was devastation and loss. All the windows on the northwest side of the house had been broken.

"There's one good thing," Mom consoled them. "It's still early enough to replant. In six weeks from now, no one should be able to tell that a storm went through here. Now let's go in and eat supper."

7

New Buggy

"HERE, Lassie," called Henry. He whistled and snapped his fingers.

Lassie got up from resting in the shade of a spreading yew shrub.

"Good dog!" He patted her head. "Sit down." He and Lassie were inseparable companions, and he had already taught her to shake-a-paw and obey simple commands.

It was Saturday just after lunch, and the four boys were resting in the grass under the maple tree.

Jeremiah, the rooster, and his hens, were scratching for insects in the barnyard. A bumblebee buzzed around them, then droned away.

Omar looked at his pocket watch. "Just five more minutes, then I'm heading for the *Schwimmeblatz* (swimming hole)," he announced. "It feels like it's ninety in the shade."

"Me too," chorused Steven and Henry.

Dad had taught them to wait awhile after eating lunch before going into the water, to lessen the risk of cramps. When Omar's watch had ticked off promised time, the three boys sauntered off toward the creek.

Joe pulled his straw hat down over his face, hoping to catch a few winks of sleep. The chirping of the seventeen-year locusts and the singing of the purple martins made him feel drowsy.

High on her perch in the maple tree, Nancy finally relaxed. While Joe had been lying on his back, she had hardly dared to move, for fear she would be seen. She reached around the trunk of the tree, and from a hole she took her diary and pen. Nancy slipped the diary out of the plastic bag she used to keep out moisture, opened to today's date, and wrote:

Dear Diary,

How I love dear Whispering Brook Farm and all its folks. I love the fields all around me. I like to whisper my secrets to the trees. I love the dear,

dear brook. I love Mammi because she is so understanding, and Daadi because he is my friend. I love Mamm because she is kind and good, and Daed because he works hard and provides for us. I love Mary because she is a lot of fun, and Joe because he calls me "Little Fairy" and tweaks my nose. I love Omar because he understands why I like trees and fields and meadows and brooks, and Steven, Henry, and Susie because it's fun to play games with them. I love baby Lydia because she is soft and sweet and cuddly.

Mary came out on the porch and called, "Nancy. Nancy, come in and dry the dishes."

Nancy noiselessly scooted in the barn window and headed for the house.

Joe got up from his nap and went to the carriage shed. He slid the big door open and backed out his new buggy to wash it and make it spick-and-span for tomorrow. He and Mary and their special friends were invited to Jake and Lydiann's house for supper tomorrow night. Only Joe didn't have a girl friend yet.

He got a bucket of water and a soft cloth and brush. The wood must not be scratched. As he brushed the seat, his thoughts turned to Amelia. Soon now, he was hoping to have her sitting there on the seat beside him, laughing and chattering away. She had a light rippling laugh and delightful little ways. Joe stood there . . . dreaming. . . .

"Are you about *faddich gmacht* (finished)?"

Joe jumped. He hadn't seen his dad approaching. "Just about Daed," he replied. "I've the wheels to do yet."

"I'd like to talk to you for a few minutes." Dad leaned against the side of the buggy. "I hope you're not planning to start dating until you're a baptized member of the church. We'd like you to wait until then, at least. I think you'll be glad someday if you take my advice."

Why? thought Joe dully. He kicked at a stone in the barnyard. *The older people and the ministers just don't want us to have any fun.* But, of course he didn't say it out loud.

"And another thing," Dad went on. "We hear that you've been getting interested in Amelia Mast. Surely you know she's not really in the *Ordnung*. The ministers have worked with her to get her to keep the rules of the church, but she's not showing a very co-operative attitude. She wants to please herself, it seems."

Joe didn't say a word, but he thought plenty. *Daed and the ministers are being unreasonable. Why don't they give Amelia a chance to grow up? They can't expect a young, lively girl to dress like an old Mammi, can they?* But if he said these things out loud, Dad would think he was talking back and being disrespectful. So he merely stared at the toe of his shoe.

"Life is real, and life is earnest, Joe," Dad said softly. "It's not for serving ourselves or doing as we please. Life here on earth is just a handbreadth, and we need to use it to prepare for all eternity." He turned and went into the barn.

Joe felt a bit more thoughtful and subdued as he finished cleaning the buggy. *Maybe Daed does have a point there. But . . . well . . . it just isn't fair to judge Amelia by the way she dresses and combs her hair. After all, it's what's in the heart that counts, isn't it?* And how could he find out what she was really like if he didn't have at least a few dates with her?

He finished the buggy, then led Chief out of his

57

stall and tied him outside. He got the currycomb and brushed Chief's coat until it fairly shone. Then he got his blacksmith tools and tightened one of the horseshoes. Chief lifted his head and whinnied. A horse and carriage were coming in the lane. Lassie ran out to meet them, barking at the horse.

"Quiet, Lassie," Joe ordered. It looked like Uncle Amos and Aunt Bertha. But what in the world! Bertha was sitting on the driver's side (on the right) and had the reins. Why wouldn't Amos be driving? Maybe he wasn't feeling well.

"Hello, hello!" Dad called, coming out of the barn as Amoses drove up. "Isn't this a nice surprise! Let's unhitch, and you can stay for supper."

"Oh, no, no," protested Bertha and Amos in unison. "We really can't stay long. We must be going."

Amos soberly shared some important news. "You see, well, I'm scheduled to be at the hospital on Monday morning. I've been having chest pains, and so I'm going in for tests. The doctor thinks I'm a likely candidate for bypass surgery." He swallowed hard.

"So?" Dad was sympathetic. "That's tough. But you must be glad your condition can be helped. So that's why Bertha is driving." He nodded to his sister.

"Yes, I'm trying not to exert myself. The reason we came is because I want to ask if you'd have a boy who could help me out for a few months until I'm recovered again." He smiled at Joe. "I don't mean to ask for your best worker, the oldest one there, but how about the next one? Do you think you could spare Omar?"

"Why, yes, I think so," Dad agreed. "We'd surely like to help you out if we can. Do you want him to go along now?"

"No. If he's there by early Monday morning, that's fine. We have to be at the hospital by seven o'clock."

"Don't you want to come in and visit with Mammi and Daadi awhile? They'd appreciate it."

"I don't think we will," Bertha decided. "Elams are bringing them over for the day after tomorrow, and we can visit then. So, we'll be going again." She slapped the reins on the horse's back.

"Take care," Dad called to Amos. "We wish you the best."

8

Henner Crist's Boys

MONDAY was the first day of school. Steven, Nancy, and Henry quickly did their morning chores, then dressed in their new school clothes. They felt rather eager, for this year they were going to Misty Hollow, a one-room school run by their church. Their teacher would be Esther Beiler, an Amish girl.

Mary packed their lunch boxes with sandwiches, red beet eggs, bunches of grapes off the vine, cookies, and apples. This was the first year Omar wasn't attending school, but he was getting ready to go

away, too—to Uncle Amos's. Dad was planning to hitch Prince to the carriage, drop the scholars off at school, then drive Omar over to Amos's farm.

"Be sure to follow instructions carefully," Mom told Omar as he stood at the mirror combing his hair. "Bertha will be nice to work for, but you'll have to do your part, too." He came over to where Mom stood at the stove, holding baby Lydia in one arm, and turning the slices of mush in the frying pan with the other.

"Here, let me hold Lydia while you do that," he offered, taking the baby from her. He lifted her up, talking and crooning to her, and was rewarded with a smile and some coos, in baby language. "I'm going to miss her—all of you—so much. Two months is a long time."

"You'll be home for weekends sometimes," Mom reminded him comfortingly. "And it will be good experience for you."

"I'll write to you often," Nancy said generously. "I'll tell you all that happens on Whispering Brook Farm."

"Good for you!" Omar cheered. "Maybe that will keep me from getting homesick." He swallowed a lump in his throat as the family gathered at the breakfast table. Dad opened the Bible to Psalm 105, and read:

O give thanks unto the Lord; call upon his name: make known his deeds among the people.

Sing unto him, sing psalms unto him:
  talk of all his wondrous works.
Glory in his holy name;
    let the heart of them rejoice that seek the Lord.
        Seek the Lord and his strength:
      seek his face evermore.
Remember his marvelous works that he has done:
    his wonders, and the judgments of his mouth;
O seed of Abraham his servant,
    you children of Jacob his chosen.
He is the Lord our God:
    his judgments are in all the earth.

He laid the Bible on the stand, and they all bowed their heads to ask the blessing.

Mom passed the mush and eggs.

"It's not fair!" Steven cried. "Omar gets to go to Uncle Amos's, and I have to go to school."

"I know," Henry echoed. "I wish *I* could go, too. That would be a lot of fun."

Omar knew the boys envied him, but he wished it wouldn't be so long. He had never been away from home for more than a few days before.

"Mamm, may I go with Omar?" Susie asked. "I could dry the dishes for Aunt Bertha."

"Not this time, Susie. Aunt Bertha has to spend a lot of time with Uncle Amos at the hospital."

"You can dry the dishes for me when Nancy's not here," Mary told Susie, "if you're really that eager to dry dishes."

"And you can help me milk the cows when Omar's not here," Mom added. "Do you want to hold their tails so they don't swish them in my face?"

Now that he had to leave them, how dear the whole family seemed to Omar. He wished that things could always stay the same, nothing would have to change, no one would have to leave to work away from home. But he would be brave.

It was the first Sunday at Uncle Amos's place. Omar had walked a mile to church at Amos's neighbors. Then he hiked home again soon after dinner. He knew hardly anyone in this district. Although the boys had been friendly, he had felt a bit out of place.

Now he had the rest of the afternoon to do as he pleased. Amos and Bertha's children were all married, so it was a little lonely around there sometimes. Omar decided to go down to the creek and look for squirrels. The leaves on the trees were changing color, no longer fresh and green, and a few were already a lovely golden color. They floated down gently on the breeze, and some fell into the creek.

Omar followed the creek around a curve and heard voices. Two Amish boys about his own age sat on the creek bank with fishing rods. He could tell right away that they were twins because they looked alike.

"Hello," Omar said politely. "I don't believe I saw you boys at church."

"Nah, we like to go fishing on Sundays. Church is for the goody-goodies. Who are you anyway?"

"I'm Omar Petersheim. I'm working for Uncle Amos while he's recovering from heart surgery. What are your names?"

"I'm Eph, and he's Mony. We live on the next farm, about a quarter mile over there." Eph waved up the hill to the west.

"Eph and Mony!" Omar chuckled. "Those can't be your real names."

"Ephraim and Emanuel, then, if that suits you better," replied Eph, casting his line far out into the water. "Say, let's move down the creek, closer to the bridge. The fish aren't biting here."

Omar followed the boys. He sensed that they weren't wholesome company, but he was lonely. The very idea, playing hooky from church, and then going fishing yet, which was *verbodde* (forbidden) on Sundays. How disobedient they were!

The sound of hoofbeats and the rattle of carriage wheels could be heard on the bridge. Mony stood up to see who it was. "It's Deacon Gid!" he reported enthusiastically to Eph. "Grab some stones."

They both ducked behind some bushes. When the carriage was close to them, they fired.

Some of the stones hit the horse, and he shied to the other side of the road. The left wheels went up over a small embankment, and the carriage tilted precariously. A woman screamed. A moment later the rig was on the level again, and the frightened horse galloped on. Eph and Mony doubled over with laughter.

"That was what he deserved," Mony chortled. "Deacon Gid's always sticking his nose into our affairs. He watches us like a hawk."

"He's just an old *Heichler* (hypocrite) himself," sneered Eph. "Dad says so. He pretends to be soo-o good."

"Yeah," Mony snorted. "He doesn't want us to smoke cigarettes, but he grows tobacco. That just doesn't add up."

Omar felt sick at heart. Never before had he heard *anyone* talk so disrespectfully about leaders of the church. And now to hear it from Amish themselves!

"Well, I'd better be going. I have to start the chores early," he told the twins as he turned to leave.

"Come down to the creek again next Sunday," Mony called after him. "We'd be glad to see you."

"Yes, do that," Eph agreed. "And bring along something to eat."

"I'll see," Omar replied, "Bye." He thought, *Like fun I will. The nerve of those boys, throwing stones at Deacon Gid! They should both be punished!*

That evening as he and Aunt Bertha were doing the milking, Omar asked, "Who are those twin boys that live about a quarter mile west of here?"

"You probably mean Henner Crist's boys. They're around your age."

"Henner Crist's boys!" Omar exclaimed. That explained everything. He had heard a lot about Henner Crist's older boys already. They had already gotten into all sorts of scrapes and were disobedient and disrespectful.

"It's sad," Aunt Bertha went on. "The twins seem to be following in their older brothers' footsteps. None of them have joined church, and it seems they want to lead a wild life. Henner Crist is taking it quite hard, but I can't help but think that it's partly his fault.

"Our Rachel worked for them before she was married, when Crist's Anna wasn't well. She said hardly a day passed that Crist didn't have something belittling and downgrading to say about those in the ministry. And whenever his boys got into trouble, he took their side and defended them. I feel sorry for the boys."

"Who is Deacon Gid?" Omar wondered. He poured some milk into a dish for the cats, then settled down beside Bossy on the milk stool. Omar liked to hear the steady swish, swish, swish of milk streaming into the pails.

"Deacon Gid read the text at church today. You would have seen him. He lives on the farm west of Henner Crist's. He's tried his best to help those boys, but they just make *Schpott* (fun, mockery) of him. It really is sad." Aunt Bertha lifted her apron and wiped a few tears from her eyes.

9

The Shack

On Monday when Omar came into the house for dinner, there was a letter for him, propped up on the windowsill. He recognized Nancy's neat, rounded handwriting. As Aunt Bertha finished mashing the potatoes and dishing up the beef, gravy, and vegetables, he sat at the table to read it.

Dear Omar,
    Hello. How do you like working at Uncle Amos's? Do you have to work hard? We miss you very

much. On Thursday evening Lassie and I went to fetch the cows, and down by Whispering Brook we found Daisy with a new little baby calf! It's so cute. I wish you could see it. We named it Bluebell.

This is the second week we're going to school at Misty Hollow. Esther Beiler is a good teacher, but she can be quite bossy sometimes. Lonnie Ray snapped a wad of paper with his suspenders, and she made him stand in a corner.

Mary invited her friends to come for supper on Sunday evening, and Jacob was here, too. When he was passing the gravy boat, it slipped out of his hands, and a lot of gravy spilled on the tablecloth. His face got red. I didn't want to laugh, but I couldn't help it. We've been teasing Mary about "*dabbich* (clumsy) Jeckie" ever since.

I think Joe's soon going to ask a girl. I flattened out a wad of paper from his bedroom wastebasket and saw "Amelia Mast" written on it and a heart drawn around it. I hope he does start dating.

Baby Lydia had to go to the clinic for a shot yesterday and is real cranky today. Steven and Henry told me to write that they say "Hi" to you. Mom, Mary, and Susie send their love, too.

> Bye for now,
> Nancy

Omar felt a wave of homesickness. Reading about the folks at home made him long to be there and see them all again. It was rather lonesome here, and he was looking forward to Uncle Amos coming home.

The rest of the week, time dragged for Omar. Finally Sunday came, the day Uncle Amos was discharged from the hospital. After the morning chores were done, Aunt Bertha told him to move the big old-fashioned rocker from the sitting room to the kitchen, and then he could do whatever he wanted until she came home with Amos. She had hired a neighbor lady to drive her to the hospital, and they would bring Amos home.

This Sunday there were no church services in Uncle Amos's district. Omar got a stack of old *Family Life* and *Young Companion* magazines and stretched out on the sofa to read. The grandfather clock in the corner ticked loudly. After he tired of reading, he dozed off awhile. Then he wandered around, feeling bored.

Omar wished he'd be at home—there was always something to do at home and someone to play a game with. After what seemed like a long, long time, he heard the sound of a car in the drive. Aunt Bertha helped Uncle Amos walk to the house. Omar held open the door for them.

"Hi, Omar," he said cheerfully. "Glad to see you." He eased himself into the rocker. "My, I'm tired." He leaned back and closed his eyes.

Aunt Bertha prepared a quick meal. After dinner, a few of their married children came to visit. Omar wondered what he could do. He felt bored and restless and was tempted to go down to the creek as Henner Crist's boys had invited him to do. His conscience bothered him, though. He knew he shouldn't associate with rowdy boys like they were.

"But I wouldn't join in any of their pranks," he argued with himself. "I've had such a boring forenoon." After battling with his conscience awhile, he decided to go. "Maybe I can be a good influence on them," he told himself. He got a bag in the washhouse, filled it with apples and pretzels, then headed for the creek.

The twins were fishing at almost the same spot where they had been last week.

"See, I told you he'd come," Mony cried.

"Yeah! He has more backbone than I thought he had!" Eph clapped him heartily on the back. They were treating him like an old friend, and Omar forgot his moment of indignation at the rousing welcome they gave him. It was good to feel wanted.

"Good, you brought some grub," Mony noticed. "Let's go over to the shack to eat it."

They followed a cow path up the wooded hillside where the trees were thickest, and through some tangled underbrush. Behind a screen of tangled vines, partially hidden from view, stood the shack. It was surprisingly well built, with real glass in the windows, a few old chairs, and a table. On the floor was an old carpet. Shelves were built along one wall, and centered on the table stood a kerosene lamp.

"Say, this is neat." Omar admired it all.

"Just wait till we get our TV set yet," Eph boasted. He reached up on the shelf and got down a pack of cards. "Let's have some fun. Too bad Deacon Gid isn't here."

Omar found himself getting used to the way the twins talked. He even laughed at the disparaging remarks they made about Deacon Gid and all Amish in general. According to these boys, most Amish were self-righteous, or *Heichler* (hypocrites), or trying to take advantage of others in business deals, or goody-goodies. Gradually, without realizing what was happening, Omar was being influenced by their talk and losing respect for his own people, too.

When it was time to start chores, Omar reluctantly got up to go. He had really enjoyed the afternoon.

"See ya next Sunday," Eph called after him.

"Nope, not next Sunday. I'm going home next weekend. But I'll see you in two weeks."

"Righto." The twins both waved good-bye.

10

Back Home

My, it was good to be home. Omar could hardly believe how things had changed. The silo filling had been done, and the fields were bare again. The trees in the meadow had bright splashes of red and gold. Nancy and Steven came running from the house to greet him. "Look what came for you, Omar." Nancy held out a wide envelope.

"Hmmmm. Mr. Omar Petersheim. Now who could this be from?" He eagerly tore it open and took out a pretty card with red roses on front and the

words "Happy Birthday" above. Inside he found neat handwriting.

To my new friend,
Happy birthday.
Hope to see you again sometime.
Love,
Jewell Vaneski

"My birthday?" Omar was amazed that he had forgotten all about it. Wednesday had been the eighteenth. So he was fifteen years old now. He stuffed the card into his shirt pocket. Never before had he received a card from a girl, and he was a bit embarrassed.

"Come and see Bluebell," Nancy begged, tugging at his arm. Dad and Mary were milking. Joe and Henry were doing the feeding. Everyone was glad to see him, and he was happy to be home. Even the barn sounds and odors were familiar and comforting.

Mom came to the barn with Susie and baby Lydia. "My, I believe you grew an inch!" his mother exclaimed. "And you need a haircut badly."

Omar grinned self-consciously. Joy filled his heart at being with those he loved best. He took baby Lydia from Mom and held her close. So soft and sweet and fragrant she was. How he had missed them all!

Surrounded by the love of his family, Henner

Crist's twins seemed remote, of little value as buddies. Now memory of their disrespectful talk repulsed him. Calling Amish people hypocrites and self-righteous—the very idea! He knew his parents weren't hypocrites. They were sincere, genuine Christians.

Grandma and Grandpa were invited over for supper, and Mom had made all of Omar's favorite foods. For dessert, Mary had made shoofly pie and homemade vanilla ice cream. She stuck a few candles in the pie and lighted them, and everyone sang "Happy Birthday" for Omar.

He felt his eyes getting misty. Being away for awhile made the family seem even more precious to him. He felt sorry for people like Jewell Vaneski; her parents were never home, and she had no brothers and sisters. Maybe he should send her a birthday card, too. She had said her birthday was September twenty-fifth.

As if reading his thoughts, Steven asked, "Who was that birthday card from, anyway?"

Omar tried to act nonchalant. "Just an *englisch* girl who came for eggs one time. I'm surprised she remembered." He felt uncomfortable when he saw Dad raise his eyebrows.

"Omar has an *Aldi,* an *Aldi* (girlfriend)!" Susie sang out, "See, he's getting pink."

That little brat! thought Omar. *She sure is getting sassy.*

"Hush, Susie," Mom gently warned her. "Was it

the one living on the Cooper place? I hear she's been trying to make friends with the Amish."

"Yes, that's the one. I'd forgotten all about her. She must be lonely."

"She's probably back in school now," Mary commented as she cut the pie. "That'll likely cure her loneliness."

"No, she doesn't go to school, according to the women at the quilting last week," Mom replied. "Her parents don't approve of the high schools around here, so she has a tutor come to her home to teach her. No wonder she's hungry for the company of young people her own age."

Omar thought he knew how Jewell must feel. He remembered how he'd yielded to temptation by joining Henner Crist's twins last Sunday. Well, they wouldn't see him next Sunday, after all. He'd made up his mind not to associate with them anymore.

Mammi pulled Omar's ears gently and counted to fifteen. He wouldn't hold still like that for anyone else, but since it was Mammi, he felt honored.

"It doesn't seem so long ago that *I* was fifteen." Daadi was having another flashback. "That summer I was kicked by a horse and spent most of the summer in bed. I had a bruised liver."

"That must've been seventy years ago," Omar calculated. "How could such a long time seem 'not so long ago'?" He shook his head in amazement.

"Let me tell you this," his grandpa went on, "even though you should live to be ninety, when

76

you look back over your life, you'll say it didn't seem long. The important thing is to live for Christ, so that when death's call comes, you'll be ready, whether at age twenty or ninety."

Later, the family was to think back to those words. But right then, with the household joyfully gathered together, and life so sweet and good, thoughts of parting seemed far away.

Sunday evening there was no singing and nothing planned for the young folks. The day had been as warm as summer.

"Say, could we eat our supper down by Whispering Brook?" begged Nancy, her eyes dancing. "It might be our last chance before it gets too cool. May we, Mamm?"

"Well, I guess we could if we do our chores first," consented Mom. "That is, if you'll help make the sandwiches and pack the basket."

Nancy, happy and flushed, rushed around slicing bread and meat and cheese. Joe was home for a change, and Omar too. How she wished no one would ever leave. But she was going to make use of their time together.

She put a pack of large marshmallows, matches, and a few newspapers in the basket. Nancy wanted a small bonfire, and Mary had promised that she and Jacob would join them, too, and they would sing. Jacob had a good voice for singing.

Finally everything was ready, and she waited impatiently for the menfolk to finish the evening chores. It was a perfect evening. The hollyhocks by the barnyard wall were gorgeous, and the row of yellow and gold marigolds along the garden flaunted their bright autumn colors. Killing frost had not yet come.

Mom had been right. The effects of the hailstorm were no longer visible, and they had harvested plenty of corn, string beans, lima beans, and tomatoes to can. The south field was dotted with large orange pumpkins.

Finally everyone was ready. The children ran on ahead to find the perfect spot for their picnic. Nancy knew just where it was—where the water whispered. They spread the tablecloth between two large trees and set out the food. As they bowed their heads to ask the blessing, Nancy listened carefully. Perhaps when everyone was quiet, she could hear the whispering of the brook. But a breeze was rustling the leaves and drowned out the murmur of the water.

"Say, this *is* a nice spot," confirmed Dad as he selected a sandwich. "I guess we should all take time to enjoy the beauties of nature more, as Nancy does. It's God's handiwork."

Warmth encircled Nancy's heart. It gave her a good feeling to be understood. Sometimes she felt as though she was being branded as peculiar for loving trees and brooks and meadows. But God had created them, and they made her feel close to God.

After they had eaten, Steven and Henry went to gather wood and twigs for the fire. Joe lay on his back and lifted baby Lydia above him. He soon had her laughing out loud as he played with her.

"There comes Jacob!" Susie called. Sure enough, his up-headed horse was trotting in the lane. A few minutes later, he and Mary came strolling through the meadow to join them.

"Come, join the circle," Dad called to them. "Looks like they want to toast some marshmallows."

"Sounds good to me," Jacob replied, seating himself on the blanket beside Joe. Mom had cleared away the remains of the meal and shaken the crumbs off the tablecloth for the ants. Mary had declared that she didn't want any supper, that a few toasted marshmallows would be enough for her, and Jacob had eaten supper at home.

As the family gathered around the fire, talking and toasting marshmallows, Omar sat back against the trunk of a tree. This scene was so beautiful, all being together like this. And it was such a beautiful summerlike evening. Dusk was descending over the peaceful countryside. There was a spicy, woodsy smell from the trees, and the breezes were friendly and caressing. A large orange moon was coming up over the horizon. Dear Whispering Brook Farm! Where the people were friendly, and there was love and kindness for all.

Omar's thoughts again turned to Jewell. What

was she doing tonight? Maybe all alone in that big house with the servants. And Henner Crist's twins? Were they perhaps at this very moment bad-mouthing the Amish? Or playing a mean prank, or watching TV in their shack? Omar suddenly felt sorry for them. How could he help them?

"Will you start a song for us, Jacob? We'll all join in and help."

In his rich, baritone voice, Jacob began, and the whole family joined in.

Ringe recht, wenn Gottes Gnade
* Dich nun ziehet und bekehrt. . . .*
Struggle well, if God's grace
  Now moves and changes you. . . .

Ringe, denn die Pfort ist enge,
* Und der Lebensweg ist schmal. . . .*
Struggle, for the gate is narrow,
  And the way to life is small. . . .

They sang a few more German hymns. Then Jacob began a favorite for outdoor gatherings, "How Great Thou Art." Their voices mingled joyfully in expressing wonder for God's creation of worlds, stars, thunder, birds, and trees. They praised God for displaying his power all through the universe and bringing salvation through Christ.

A feeling of peace and contentment filled Omar's heart as he sang and listened to the beautiful words and tunes. The mixed-up feelings that Eph and Mony's talk had created in his heart were no longer there. God seemed close. "How Great Thou Art" was so fitting to sing out here under the trees, by Nancy's Whispering Brook.

11

Love

JOE struck a match and lit the kerosene lamp beside his bed. He reached into the bureau drawer for his tablet and pen—he had an important letter to write. When had he last written a letter? Probably not since he was in school, composing an English assignment.

"Dear Amelia," he wrote. *If only I'd have better handwriting*, he thought.

"If it's all right with you, I'd like to take you home from the singing on Sunday evening."

Now what could he write next, or how could he

word it? He sat staring into space. He remembered the talk Dad had with him, that Saturday afternoon when he was washing the buggy. Dad had advised him not to date any girl until he was a church member. Joe had thought things over carefully and decided to ignore his dad's advice. After all, his father had not strictly forbidden him to go out with a girl.

What if someone else asked Amelia before he did, and she accepted him? He shuddered. What an unbearable thought! He was old enough to make his own decisions now, and he was sure that Amelia was the one for him, even though Daed didn't think so. Anyway, how could he find out if he didn't date her?

He decided to start over with the letter. "Dear Amelia, may I take you home from the singing on Sunday evening?"

No, that didn't sound right either. Someone was coming up the steps. Quickly he crumpled the letter and tossed it into the wastebasket. Joe thought about asking Mary to write the letter. But no, she might try to persuade him not to write to Amelia. He took out a fresh piece of paper and began again.

Dear Amelia,

I would like to take you home from the singing on Sunday evening. Please let me know whether or not I may.

        Sincerely,
        Joe Petersheim

It didn't sound right at all, but he was too tired to try again. He slipped it into an envelope, sealed it, stamped it, and put Amelia's name and address on it. There it was, for better or worse. He slipped it under some other things in the top bureau drawer, then retrieved the crumpled sheet from the waste can, took it downstairs, and popped it into the cookstove. Mom gave him a wondering look but said nothing.

The week seemed to drag. It wouldn't be possible for him to receive a reply from her before Thursday, but he watched the mail anyway.

On Thursday morning Joe was busy cleaning out the stables and hauling manure. Mom and Mary were cleaning out the garden, since a killing frost was expected before long. He hoped they would finish before the mail came, or Mary would be the first to reach the mailbox. He didn't want her to see any letter from Amelia.

At eleven o'clock Joe unhitched the horses and put them into the barn. He would offer to help the women in the garden before the noon meal, and then he would be handy to fetch the mail when the carrier stopped.

"Need help?" he asked, walking over to where Mom and Mary had filled bushel baskets with carrots and beets to be put into the cellar.

"Good for you." Mom was grateful. "I should go in and start dinner. You can help Mary carry these into the cellar."

"Those muscles of yours sure come in handy." Mary laughed. "And it was so nice of you to offer. There's a girl out there somewhere who will be lucky to get you."

"Aw, cut it out," Joe protested. He felt a little guilty about his reason for offering to help. Just then he spied the familiar blue mail car coming up the road. "I'll get it," he quickly said. His heart skipped a beat when he saw a lavender-flowered envelope in the box, with his name on it. Amelia's letter!

Trembling with excitement, he stuffed the letter into his pocket. Luckily, Mary had her back turned and didn't see it. Although he was bursting with curiosity, he helped Mary with the garden things until dinner was ready. At the table, Joe felt almost too excited to eat. As soon as they had returned thanks after the meal, he slipped upstairs. With trembling fingers he tore open the envelope and read the message.

Dear Joe,

Thank you for your letter, which I received today. I would be glad to have you take me home from the singing on Sunday evening. I am looking forward to keeping company with you.

Lieb (love),
Amelia

Joe's heart filled with gladness. Suddenly he felt like singing and laughing and crying at the same time. She had said yes! She called him *dear,* and she signed with *Lieb!*

He reread the letter several times. What elegant, flowery handwriting she had. Just three more days! If only he could somehow make those days go faster.

12

Pranks

THE week was dragging for Omar, too. The newness of working for Uncle Amos had worn off. His weekend at home had made things worse instead of better. He felt blue and homesick—how he wished he could be at home. Sunday finally arrived, but it was another boring day. There was no church in their district.

Uncle Amos and Aunt Bertha had some visitors, both in the forenoon and in the afternoon, but no one Omar's age. He remembered he had told the

twins that he would be there today. Maybe he should go, to keep his word. The more he toyed with the idea, the more it appealed to him. "I'll try to help them," he told himself. Then he was off.

The twins hailed him gladly. "So you were man enough to come," Mony praised him. "We had about decided you must've chickened out."

It was amazing how different Omar felt when he was with the twins. Soon he was laughing at their jokes and even joining their style, poking fun at the teams that occasionally passed.

"Look at that poky old horse," Eph mocked, doubling over with laughter. "His nose is almost down to the ground."

"So is his belly," Mony joined in. "Doesn't that look pathetic!"

"Say, I have a super idea," Eph eagerly proposed. "Deacon Gid is visiting in Summerville for the day. He won't be home till late. We could go over there and do some of his chores for him."

Mony stared at him for a moment before he understood. "Wow, that's a great scheme. Let's go! He deserves it."

Omar tagged along, too, even though he guessed the type of things they were planning to do. He remembered how he had reasoned that he could somehow help them. Now was the time.

Yet Eph was telling him to hurry. He knew it would be useless to say anything anyway.

"You aren't going to be a goody-goody, are

you?" Mony challenged him.

That clinched it. Omar fell into step with them.

At Deacon Gid's dairy barn, Eph grabbed the milk pails and hid them inside the milk cooler. Mony took the strainer and threw it into the cow gutter.

"Aren't you going to help do the chores?" he asked Omar, who was standing there watching. "Get busy."

Omar grabbed a shovel, went outside, and hoisted it onto the shanty roof over the diesel which generated power to run the milkers and the milk cooler. Suddenly he heard the sound of a horse and carriage coming up the road. He yanked open the door of the shanty and quickly stepped inside, pulling the door shut after him.

The horse was slowing down, and he heard the driver say "Whoa!"

Omar's heart thumped loudly. Footsteps passed the diesel shanty and went into the barn. A few minutes passed.

"That's strange," he heard a man saying on the way out of the barn. "I thought I saw someone outside the barn door a minute ago, but there's no one around now. . . . Giddap!" The horse trotted on down the road.

Omar opened the door a crack and peeked out. The carriage was no longer in sight. Stealthily he crept into the barn. "Boys," he called.

Eph's head appeared above the feed bin, and Mony crawled out from behind some hay bales.

"Hey, that was a close shave," Eph cried. "We'd better finish quick and do this job right." He grabbed a sack of cow feed, opened it, and poured it into the gutter as he walked along. Mony did the same with another bag.

Omar gasped. This was getting to be more than a harmless prank. They were deliberately destroying someone else's property! He didn't want to have anything more to do with it.

"Come quick!" he hissed urgently. "Someone might come in here any minute."

The boys tossed their empty sacks on the floor and followed Omar. "That ought to teach him a lesson," Mony crowed triumphantly, "for always watching us like a hawk. Why doesn't he do something about all those self-righteous hypocrites instead of picking on us."

Omar was walking as fast as he could. "Hey, what's your big hurry, anyway?" panted Eph. "I can hardly keep up. You aren't afraid, are you?"

"Afraid of what?" asked Omar. "I didn't damage anything. I'm just in a hurry to get back to do the chores for Uncle Amos." He hoped he wasn't telling a lie.

"Well, just so you don't go and tattle on us!" warned Mony. "We took you for a buddy. Now don't go and turn traitor on us, just because we played a few pranks on someone. Promise you won't?"

"Of course, I won't."

"Well, that's good. Anyone who tattles on us gets

beaten black and blue. Right, Eph?"

"You'd better believe it," Eph declared.

The boys parted at the bridge, and Omar followed the creek home to Uncle Amos's. He was determined to stay away from the twins after this.

Omar went to bed early on Sunday evening. He was tired, and he wanted to forget about the day's happenings. It seemed like he had just fallen asleep, when he was awakened by the ferocious barking of the dog. "What could be wrong now?" he muttered, groping in the dark for his pants.

As he passed the window, something caught his eye. He stopped, horrified. Fire! Angry flames were shooting into the sky, in the west, lighting up the countryside!

"Henner Crist's barn!" Omar gulped, wide awake now. He dashed down the steps and grabbed his flashlight from the table. A moment later Aunt Bertha appeared at the bedroom door, looking almost like a frightened ghost in her big white nightgown and nightcap.

"There's a fire to the west," Omar stated, in a low urgent voice. "Do you mind if I go over to see where it is?"

"Oh, dear!" Aunt Bertha looked as if she were ready to cry. "I guess you might as well go. Do be careful, though."

Omar was off in a flash. He forgot to put on his

shoes, but he grabbed his hat and jacket. The closest route over was along the creek. Omar ran blindly, stumbling, falling, rising again. As soon as he reached the bridge, he saw that the fire was not at Henner Crist's, as he had guessed, but at Deacon Gid's.

In the distance he heard the wail of the fire sirens, getting closer. What a relief! At least help was coming. A small crowd of neighbors had already gathered when Omar arrived, breathless and panting.

It was the tobacco shed that was burning. He watched as angry flames crept up the sides of the roof. Within minutes flames began to shoot through the shingled roof. Big puffs of black smoke billowed up into the murky sky.

Omar couldn't keep himself from shivering. The faces of those standing around watching seemed to flicker in the eerie light of the flames. The fire trucks had arrived, and the yellow-clad firemen were busily setting up to get some water on the fire.

"I'm afraid it's too late to save the tobacco shed," one of the Amish spectators was saying. "But I wish they'd hurry and shoot some water on the house and the dairy barn. The wind's from the east. At least the cows are in the meadow, and there's no stock in the tobacco shed."

"Do you have any idea what started the fire?" someone else asked.

"No, I don't, but," the first man said, lowering his

voice confidentially, "this afternoon as I was coming home and passing here, I thought I saw someone outside the barn door. I stopped in and looked around, but whoever it was had disappeared."

"Do you think someone did it on purpose, I mean, set fire to it?" The voice expressed doubt.

"What else? There was no storm, no electric in the shed, no overheated hay."

Omar felt sick at heart. He didn't want to hear more, and he edged farther away from them. The fire was now a thunderous roar, like a huge monster, and the rafters and walls of the shed seemed to melt under the attack of the ravenous flames.

Another Amish man joined the group. Omar couldn't hear as clearly now, what they were saying, but he perked up his ears when he heard "saw them going into the barn." Then the words, "Henner Crist's twin boys and that Petersheim boy that's working for Amos while he's laid up."

He didn't wait for more. Trying not to attract attention, he moved to the opposite edge of the crowd, then headed for home. Reaching the bridge, Omar jumped over the fence and into the meadow. Tears were streaming down his cheeks, tears of anger and frustration. So they were blaming him and the twins for having set fire to the tobacco shed. The very nerve! If only he hadn't gone with those mischief-makers. But it was too late now.

He sneaked into the kitchen, hoping Aunt Bertha wouldn't hear him. He didn't want to face anyone now. Stealthily he crept up the stairs and crawled under the covers. If only it would just have been a bad dream, and he would wake up to find that it hadn't really happened. He tossed and turned. More than anything else, he wanted to go home to Dad and Mom. He thought of pretending to be sick. But, no, that would be dishonest.

Maybe he could persuade Joe to take his place, now that the silo filling was done. But that would arouse suspicion for sure. There was no way out of his dilemma. If only he could somehow clear his name. But there was no way he could prove anything. He had been there with the twins that afternoon, he couldn't deny that. Finally Omar fell into a troubled sleep, only to be awakened by terrifying dreams of the fire—and of his accusers, pointing at him and crying, "Guilty! Guilty! Away with him! Away with him!"

The next few days were grim for Omar. His appetite failed, and he could hardly choke down the food Aunt Bertha prepared. But he forced himself to eat a nearly normal amount and to act cheerful. He knew that if Uncle Amos and Aunt Bertha heard the rumor, they could be suspecting him of arson. If he acted sick, they might even believe he set the fire. As days went by and he heard nothing more of it, he began to relax a bit.

The morning of the shed raising dawned bright and clear. At the breakfast table, Uncle Amos told Omar, "If you hurry with the chores, you can be one of the first ones there. I know you're looking forward to it."

"I'll milk the cows alone," Aunt Bertha generously offered.

"No, I'll help," Omar quickly replied.

He thought, *I wish we'd have a hundred cows to milk, so I wouldn't have to go to the shed raising.* He wondered what Amos and Bertha would think if they knew how he dreaded it. He tried to dream up some excuse to stay away that wouldn't look suspicious. Perhaps he could play hooky and stay in the woods all day, but then Uncle Amos would ask him how the raising went and who all was there and how much they got done. No, there was just no way out. He'd have to go.

Dozens of teams were passing by as Omar reached the bridge. Men in two-wheeled carts, spring wagons, and trottin' buggies. Families in market wagons and carriages.

When Omar arrived, he looked around for someone he knew. He noticed that Henner Crist's twins were nowhere to be seen. Omar joined the group of boys he had met at church. Did they eye him a bit cooly, or did he just imagine it? He felt ill at ease.

Soon excitement began as the frames were raised. Using ropes and long spiked poles, the men and boys tugged and pushed each section into place. The sound of hammering could be heard from all over the shed. At ten o'clock the girls set up a table under a tree for treats. The men were working hard and needed fuel for energy. Platters of sandwiches, bowls of potato chips, plates of doughnuts, and cups of hot chocolate and coffee were set out.

Omar hadn't eaten much breakfast, and he was really thirsty, so he followed the other boys to the table. As he reached for a cup of hot chocolate, he heard one of the girls giggle. She was whispering to a friend beside her, and Omar clearly heard the words, "Yes, that's the one. Joe's brother."

He looked up sharply. Both girls were looking at him. Omar turned away, no longer hungry. So even the girls were talking about him, pointing him out as the one who helped set fire to the tobacco shed. Tears blinded his eyes as he walked off. He wouldn't stay another minute.

Poor Omar! He didn't know the girls were Joe's Amelia and her friend. They had heard no rumor about him and were merely identifying him as Joe's brother.

Omar forced himself to walk calmly, even though he wanted to run. What a relief when he reached the bridge and could slip into the obscurity of the woods, where there was no chance of meeting anyone.

Almost without thinking, he followed the path up the wooded hillside. Omar didn't want to go home yet. He knew Uncle Amos and Aunt Bertha would ask him why he hadn't stayed for dinner.

Suddenly he stopped in his tracks. Was that music he was hearing? Then it dawned on him. He was near the twins' shack.

Omar stood undecided for a few minutes, then strode ahead. He had nowhere else to go, anyway. Omar knocked on the door, and the music stopped. The door opened slowly, and Mony stuck his head out.

"Hurrah, it's Omar!" he cried, smiling broadly and clapping Omar on the back. "Welcome to the shack. Come in!" He kicked the door wide open.

"Come in, old buddy," Eph called. "Want to listen to some radio music?"

"No, let's talk," Mony objected. "Say, Omar, did you hear that they're blaming us twins for setting fire to Gid's tobacco shed?"

"Not just you!" Omar complained. "They're blaming me, too."

"It just goes to show what unfair, unreasonable, stupid, self-righteous *Heichler* (hypocrites) they are."

Omar detected the hatred in Eph's words as he spat them out, and he realized that Eph's feelings matched his own.

"Ya well, I'm just not going to let it bother me," Mony declared as he stamped on the floor.

After that, Omar and the twins were inseparable companions. While Omar was still working for Uncle Amos, they spent every Sunday together.

The twins' attitude about the Amish was rubbing

off on Omar, and he found himself agreeing with everything they said. He knew his parents and grandparents were sincere, honest people, but they were exceptions. They were just a few good apples in a basket of rotten ones.

13

Full Moon

AT the singing on Sunday evening, Joe drove up to the front walk and reined in Chief. Where was Amelia? In a moment he heard her tinkling laugh. With the reins in hand, he stepped out of the buggy, and she appeared from the darkness, swishing past him, climbing in. A whiff of perfume enveloped him as he stepped in the buggy after her.

Given free rein, Chief took off down the lane. A few whistles and catcalls followed them, as was customary when a new couple paired off.

"My, it's chilly," Amelia observed, shivering. "It feels like winter's coming."

"It usually is colder over the time of the full moon," Joe commented, tucking in the buggy robe.

"Oh, is it full moon tonight? How romantic!" Amelia gushed.

Joe had hardly dared look at Amelia yet. Just having her here on the seat beside him was almost bewildering for him. But now their eyes met.

"Just right for our first date," she added, with eyes sparkling in the moonlight.

They were silent for a few moments. Then Amelia broke the spell by asking, "Did you hear that Ben D's are having a husking bee the last Wednesday in October? I can hardly wait."

"Yes, that will be fun," Joe agreed. "There haven't been many of those lately."

"I hope we get to work together," Amelia said enthusiastically. "It would be so much more fun that way."

It was only a few miles to Amelia's aunt and uncle's place, Cookie Dan's, as everyone called their farm. While they were driving in the tree-lined lane, Chief suddenly shied, then stopped. He snorted, and his nostrils flared. A dark shape moved off into the darkness.

"Wh—what was that?" Amelia's teeth were chattering.

A moment later they heard a soft moo, then another, and the sound of running hoofbeats in the lane. "*Die Kieh sin aus* (the cows are out)!" Amelia cried shrilly.

The whole herd seemed to be trotting toward them now. Chief snorted loudly, again and again, then reared up into the air. In a moment Joe was at his head, calming and soothing him. A dog was barking furiously from the barn, and a light went on in the kitchen. At the sight of Joe's rig, the cows had turned around again, and Amelia jumped off the buggy, shouting and chasing them.

She's not quite so ladylike now, Joe thought, chuckling. The sight of her running after the cows amused him. With the help of Dan and his wife, the cows were soon safely corralled in the barnyard.

"We'll never forget this, how the cows were out on our first date, will we?" Amelia was giggling as she led the way into the house. She struck a match, lit the Aladdin lamp, turned it low, then drew the shades.

It was an enchanting evening for Joe, and he whistled a happy tune while driving home after midnight. *Dad really wasn't fair to judge Amelia by the way she dressed,* he told himself. After all, she wasn't stuck-up. She was lots of fun, and good-natured too.

She had such fascinating little ways that stirred his heart. In fact, Amelia was everything Joe had ever wanted in a girl. He was sure Dad would change his mind about her once he got to know her better. Amelia was really special, and he was very, very lucky to be her beau.

Nancy smiled to herself as she sat in the kitchen rocking baby Lydia to sleep. At the stove, Mom was stirring the kettle of mush. Dad was reading the farm paper, Mary was icing a cake, Susie was playing, and the boys were having a lively discussion about guinea pigs in the other end of the kitchen.

Everything was all right again because Omar was finally at home to stay. All the time he was gone, she had felt a sense of loss, that something wasn't as it should be.

Mom took a big pan of apple dumplings out of the oven and set it on the table.

"Come, everyone, sit down," she called. "Supper's ready."

No one needed a second invitation. The family bowed their heads to silently ask the blessing, then dished out the food.

"Mush and milk!" Omar exclaimed in delight. "Mamm, I didn't have any all the time I was away."

"Yes, eat your fill of it. You've lost weight." Mom's voice sounded concerned.

"Didn't Bertha cook good enough for you, or did she work you too hard?" There was a twinkle in Dad's eyes as he spoke.

Omar felt a warmth encircling his heart. It was so good to be home and to sense the loving care of his family.

"I'll bet he missed us all so much that he could

hardly eat," teased Joe.

"Were you really that homesick?" Nancy asked, wide-eyed.

"Of course he wasn't," Mary defended him. "I know how it is when you're working away from home. Here, Omar, you get two apple dumplings, and everyone else gets just one."

Omar smiled his thanks. Here, in the safety and comfort of home, he could forget that he had ever been with Henner Crist's twins, and that he was accused of aiding and abetting in arson.

As if reading his thoughts, Steven asked, "Did they ever find out what caused the fire in that tobacco shed near Uncle Amos's place?"

"Nope," Omar replied, without lifting his head from his food.

"I wanted to come and help on the day of the raising." Dad was pouring milk over his dumpling. "But it was the only day it suited for them to bring out concrete for the manure yard. I suppose you were there, though."

"Yes, Daed, I was there" Omar tried desperately to think of what to say, to change the subject quickly. He was afraid they'd find out that he had left early.

"Say, is it true, what Susie said about Joe?" Luckily Omar had thought of something.

"Of course it's true." Susie was indignant. "I don't tell lies. Joe, tell him it's true that you have an *Aldi* (girlfriend)."

Joe nodded and shifted uncomfortably in his

chair. It was still a touchy subject. He knew he didn't have his parents' approval, although they hadn't said anything more since he had started dating Amelia. He was thankful for that.

There was a tap-tap-tapping sound of Daadi's cane, and the door to the grandparents' kitchen opened.

"Well, I see that Omar's home," Mammi remarked, smiling. "I guess we'll stay and visit awhile."

"Yes, please do that." Mom pulled up the rocker for Daadi. Maami sat on the settee, and Susie ran to her and climbed on her lap.

A mysterious contentment flooded Omar's heart. *Home, sweet home,* he thought happily. *Be it ever so humble, there's no place like home.*

14

Cornhusking

JACOB Yoder urged his horse to go faster. It was the evening of the corn husking at Ben D's, and he was on his way to pick up Mary. The sun was setting in a maze of gray and pink. It was a beautiful evening.

When Jacob turned off Covered Bridge Road, he could see the buildings of the Petersheim farm—or rather, the Whispering Brook Farm. That sign up there on the barn never failed to get a chuckle out of him. What a dear family the Petersheims were!

By now King was so used to coming here that he

turned in the lane of his own accord. Jacob drove past the barn, turned around, and stopped at the walk. Mary had never kept him waiting, and neither did she tonight. There she was, smiling, *schee* (pretty), and charming as ever. King waited patiently while she got in.

"It's a perfect evening for a husking bee, isn't it?" Mary greeted him enthusiastically. "Look at that sunset."

"Yes, it reminds me of the verse in Psalms where it says, 'The heavens declare the glory of God; and the firmament shows his handiwork.' "

They watched in awe as the rosy display gradually faded in the west.

"It's hard to believe that some people actually say they don't believe there is a God," Mary commented in wonder.

"We have a neighbor who is an atheist," Jacob responded. "He says he would not believe in a God that allows so much suffering. Dad told him that suffering is a result of sin, either directly or indirectly, and that Jesus is the remedy for sin and suffering."

Mary looked at Jacob with a new respect. This was the first time they had ever had a discussion about spiritual matters. "Yes, I agree with him," she softly declared herself. "In the resurrection, the redeemed will be free of all sin and suffering."

They sat in comfortable silence, both deep in thought. The ride to Ben D's didn't seem long, and soon they were one of the stream of buggies, their blinkers flashing, driving in the lane at Ben D's.

"There go Joe and Amelia," Jacob pointed out. "The third team ahead. By the way, what do your parents think of his choice by now?"

"You mean Amelia? They aren't exactly happy about it, but they think they've said enough. They're making it a matter of prayer."

"That may be wise." Jacob reined in King, searching for a place to tie him.

Soon they were among a group of laughing, chattering young people starting with the cornhusking. A silvery moon was rising over the field of corn shocks. The dark boughs of trees in the fence row, tossing in silhouette against the moonlit sky, added to the beauty of the evening.

"This is fun," Mary exclaimed, breathing in deeply of the fresh, clear air. "It's something I haven't done for awhile. I almost forgot how to use the husking hook."

"Same here," Jacob replied. "We put all our corn into the silos."

The couples had paired off to husk together, so Jacob and Mary were working side by side.

"It's not hard to tell where Amelia and Joe are working, is it?" Mary remarked in a low voice. "With that tinkling giggle of hers . . ."

Jacob chuckled. "It looks like she has him wrapped around her little finger."

When the husking was finished, the young folks were told to go in to the porch for treats.

"It's almost too nice to go in." Mary seemed pensive. "I'd like to walk down to the fence row. I thought I heard a screech owl a minute ago."

"Suits me," Jacob consented. They sauntered down to the trees, then sat on the split-rail fence, enjoying the beauty of the night. Suddenly they heard stealthy footsteps. A lone figure was sneaking past them on the back lane from the fields.

"Wer kann das sei (who can that be)?" Mary whispered.

"Beats me," Jacob muttered. "Looks like someone's up to mischief." The person stopped at one of the corn shocks, reached into a pocket, then crouched beside the shock. He struck a match and held it to the dry corn fodder. For an instant his face was illuminated by the light of the match, but they couldn't make out who it was. The fodder blazed, and blue flames crept up the side of the shock.

"Hey, put that out!" Jacob yelled, getting up and running toward the burning shock at top speed.

The figure raced across the field and into the darkness, without once looking back. Jacob tossed a burning bundle to the ground and tried to stamp out the fire, but it was useless. By now the whole shock was in flames. Mary ran up, breathless, but she too saw it was too late to put it out.

"Who would do such a mean thing?" she blurted out indignantly. "We had such an enjoyable time, and now someone has to go and spoil it all."

"Probably some *Naaseweis* (smart aleck), wanting adventure," Jacob surmised. "It's too bad."

The group of boys came running toward them, and the girls were not far behind.

"What happened? Who started the fire?"

Joe was one of the first ones to get there.

"We don't know. Someone ran across the field."

The flames were leaping high into the air by now, casting an eerie glow on the faces of the young people standing around watching.

"Whenever we want to have some fun, someone has to come along and spoil it all," someone muttered. "Now no one will want to hold a husking bee for the young folks."

In a few minutes, the shock had burned down to glowing embers. The boys and girls trudged back up to the house. Mary and Jacob helped themselves to popcorn and glasses of cider while chatting with Ben D and his wife. The other young people were playing party games such as skip to my Lou, six-handed reel, twin sisters, and O-Hi-O.

On the way home, the stars were still twinkling, and the moon shone with its silvery light on the young couple in the buggy. King was raring to go home, and soon they drove up the lane to Whispering Brook Farm.

"See you Sunday evening," Jacob told Mary as she stepped out of the buggy.

Mary watched Jacob drive off into the darkness, his buggy lights growing fainter and fainter in the darkness, until they were only dots. Then she turned and went into the house.

Mom had left a kerosene lamp burning on the kitchen table. Mary settled down on the rocker with the *Die Botschaft* (The News) to wait for Joe. The kitchen clock chimed twelve midnight, twelve-thirty, then one o'clock. Finally blinking buggy lights appeared, coming in the lane.

When Joe came tiptoeing in the door, Mary said in a low voice, so as not to awaken Mom and Dad, "Well, well, it surely didn't take you one and a half hours to drive home from Amelia's place. Did Chief go lame, or what happened?"

Joe winked at Mary. "Ask me no questions, and I'll tell you no lies." He grinned, took off his shoes, and went up the stairs softly.

Mary shook her head in exasperation. "I won't wait up for you again," she muttered as she headed for her room.

15

Winter Wonderland

WINTER arrived in all its grandeur and majesty. Fleecy white flakes of snow floated gently in the air, then spiraled down faster and faster, until every field, dell, and slope of the entire farm was covered with a soft, thick blanket of the beautiful stuff.

The dark green pines in the fir grove made a pretty picture, covered with fluffy white mounds of snow. In the old apple orchard, every gnarled branch and twig was bedecked with it, and beautiful drifts were all around the trees. Whispering Brook

was frozen solid and heaped high with snow between its banks.

"It looks like an old-fashioned winter storm," mused Mom, glancing out the window as she fed baby Lydia.

"As much as I love snow," lamented Mary, as she cranked the butter churn, "I wish it wouldn't have had to snow today. I'm afraid we won't be able to go to the taffy pull tonight."

The cream inside the churn went swish, swish, splash, splash, flop, flop; but there was still no butter.

"Mamm, where's Nancy?" Mary asked. "Maybe she could churn for awhile. I'm hot and tired."

"She's helping Susie make paper dolls in the sitting room," Mom replied. "Here comes Joe. He can crank the churn awhile for you."

"Don't forget to take off your boots," Mary called sharply when Joe opened the door. "I just washed the floor."

"Whew! I wish Jacob could've heard that," Joe teased. " 'Bout time he finds out how bossy you are." He grinned at Mary as he hung his gloves on the stovepipe shelf to dry."

"Well, you might be surprised at how Amelia would yell at you if you'd track dirt on her clean floor," Mary shot back. "Better get in the habit of taking your boots off now. Here, lend me a hand for a few minutes. With your strong arms, you should be able to bring on the butter in a hurry."

Mom sat baby Lydia on the floor, and Joe good-naturedly cranked the churn as he made faces at her. In return, he was rewarded with smiles and coos.

"I'm so afraid we won't be able to go to the taffy pull that it's making me cranky," Mary apologized. "I was looking forward to this party all week."

"If that's what is wrong, you can cheer up right now," Joe drawled, thumping the crank of the churn. "I'm getting the big bobsled in shape for tonight. We can take Amelia and Jacob along in it."

"Oh, you wonderful brother!" Mary clasped her hands rapturously in front of her. "Won't that be glorious fun?" But then a look of dismay crossed her face. "Oh, dear, how will I be able to let Jacob know that he won't need to pick me up? I guess I could get to the phone shack, but I don't want to bother an *englisch* neighbor to pass word on to Jacob unless it's an emergency."

But Joe had an answer for that, too. "If it keeps on snowing like this, he won't be able to come anyway. If not, we'll just go early enough, before he has time to start off. Say, if this isn't butter by now, I miss my guess." He lifted the cover off the churn.

"Sure enough, a beautiful lump of butter's floating in the buttermilk."

Mary was cheerful again, now that her problem over the taffy party was solved and the butter had come. After an early supper, they hurried with the chores, then got ready to go. Joe harnessed Chief and Prince to pull the bobsled as a team, and Mary bundled up.

"Be sure to wear both your coat and your shawl," Mom told Mary. "It's going to be a *kalt Nacht* (cold night)."

It had stopped snowing, and the air was clear and crisp. In the wintry darkness, Omar helped Joe hitch up the horses by the light of the *Ladann* (lantern) they had set on the bobsled seat. There was a strange sense of desolation in his heart. Mary and Joe were going off to have a jolly good time at the party, and he felt left out. When his family went to a gathering, he no longer enjoyed playing with the little boys.

In high spirits, Mary came skipping out and climbed on the sleigh. She sensed Omar's mood and tried to cheer him up. "Before you know it, Omar, you'll be old enough to go, too. Actually, in less than three-fourths of a year."

Then they were off, with sleigh bells ringing, and the horses tossing their heads and prancing in the snow. Omar shuffled back to the barn through the snow. A tight feeling threatened to suffocate him. After being around Henner Crist's twins so much, and being blamed for arson, he no longer had a desire to join the Amish young folks and to drive a horse. Much of the time, he felt mixed up and unhappy.

"Come and help us build a snow fort in the orchard," Steven called, throwing a snowball at Omar.

"Yes, c'mon, Omar," Henry begged. "Nancy's coming, too. Then we'll have even teams for a snowball battle."

"Nah," Omar declined. "You can play your silly game. I think I'll go for a walk." He went into the barn to hunt for a pair of snowshoes.

"I wonder what makes him so cranky the last while," Steven griped. "Ever since he got back from working at Uncle Amos's place."

"I know. It's disgusting," Henry agreed. "He's just too *grossfiehlich* (feeling big) to play with us. Someone ought to take him down a peg or two."

Omar found the snowshoes and headed for the meadow. The sky had cleared and was studded with twinkling stars, and a large silver moon was coming up behind the fir grove. The sparkling white snow was lustrous, with a path of moonlight glistening on it. Omar found himself relaxing and feeling better under the spell of such beauty and majesty.

He quickly became accustomed to walking with the snowshoes and decided to follow Whispering Brook back into the hills. The moonlit expanse of brookside meadow, in springtime covered with buttercups and forget-me-nots and violets, made it easy for him to follow the stream. Soon Omar was far out of sight of the farm buildings, back in a winter wonderland of snowy woods and fields and meadow.

He stopped to catch his breath and leaned against a tree to take in the awesome, dazzling beauty all around him. Suddenly he jerked to attention, startled to see a lone figure down by the brook and heading his way on cross-country skis.

"Hello," a girlish voice called, cheerily. "Who are

115

you?" Omar relaxed. He remembered the voice. "Is that you, Jewell?"

"That's right," she replied, laughing. "And now I see who you are. You're Omar, right?"

"Yes," he answered. Then he added, shyly, "Thanks for the birthday card you sent me."

"You're welcome. I thought a lot about you since we met and was hoping to be able to see you again. We're almost twins, remember?"

"Yes, I remember. What are you doing back here all alone?" It felt comfortable to talk with Jewell, and he found his self-confidence building.

"I was alone and tired of watching TV, and it was such a perfectly delightful evening that I had to get outside. I always come back here when I'm lonely," she added quietly. "It's so beautiful, and I feel close to God here. Just look at that lovely moon."

She lifted her face to the moonbeams, and Omar was glad, for it gave him a chance to look at Jewell. She was wearing a snowsuit, and her delicate face, glowing in the moonlight, looked more angelic than

ever. Something stirred within Omar's heart.

"Doesn't it make you feel close to God?" Jewell asked huskily, "Being at one with nature like this?"

"Yes, it does," he replied sincerely. "It soothes me."

"You've described it exactly right." Jewell had an ecstatic look on her face as she was clasping and unclasping her hands. "Skiing with God in a winter wonderland like this fills an empty place in my heart."

"It sounds like you're a believer, even though you aren't Amish," Omar said in a tone showing surprise.

"Oh, yes," she replied, smiling at him. "But I never go to church. Somehow, I'm sure I feel closer to God out here than I ever would in a church."

Omar pondered this for a moment before he continued. "But then, how did you learn about God?

Did your parents teach you?"

"No, my parents aren't Christians." There was a wistful note in her voice. "But two years ago I had a Christian governess, Mrs. Price. She led me to the Lord."

"Bu—but if you don't go to church and don't dress p—plain, how can you be sure you are a Christian?" Omar stammered awkwardly, with a note of disbelief in his voice.

Jewell glanced quickly at Omar and felt satisfied that he wasn't making fun of her. He was sincere, of that she felt sure.

"I do try to dress modestly," she assured him. "I know it's not right for a Christian to be scantily clad, and it's too cold for that tonight, anyhow. I know I'm a Christian, because I feel the Lord's presence in my heart."

After a pause, she added. "Why? Don't you feel a person can be a Christian if they aren't Amish?"

"Oh no, no, I mean yes, er . . . I don't know—," Omar broke off in confusion. "I didn't mean that you couldn't be a Christian," he finished lamely. "That's not for me to decide."

Impulsively, Jewell responded, "I wish I would have been raised as an Amish girl. I admire you people so much, with your large close-knit families, your thrifty ways, working hard and helping each other. I think it's neat. But I'd never fit in now." She shook her head from side to side.

"Sure you would. You could learn." Omar

grinned at the thought of Jewell wearing an Amish dress, prayer cap, bonnet, and shawl.

"Do you really think so?" Jewell asked, wide-eyed. "Would I be welcome at your quilting bees and singings and husking parties, or whatever the young folks do?"

"Of course, if you'd dress like the rest and try to follow the teachings of the church," Omar assured her.

Then a sudden thought sobered Omar. Could he trust her? Should he tell her what Henner Crist's twins thought? That a lot of the Amish are hypocrites and self-righteous and what not all? Should he share with her that he had no desire to join the church?

Omar wished he'd have someone with whom to unburden these bad feelings. Would Jewell be the right person to confide in? He knew he couldn't talk to his parents about it. They'd be terribly hurt and shocked. Maybe Jewell would understand.

"I know I should choose a church soon," Jewell was saying. "You people are so friendly and sincere. I wish I could be like you. But I'm afraid it's hope-less. . . . I could never fit in and learn all I'd need to." She brushed back her hair with a mittened hand.

"But surely you know that the Amish are far from perfect," Omar said pointedly. He wanted to say more, and yet he didn't want to reveal all his feel-ings.

"Yes, I know that," she agreed. "But if everyone lived like the Amish, there would be no wars, no divorces—" Her voice broke, and she brushed away a tear. "My parents are talking of divorce, and I never really had a family. . . ."

Jewell was sobbing now, and Omar looked away in embarrassment. He wished he could think of something to do or say that would comfort Jewell, but he couldn't think of anything.

"Goodness, what a big baby I am!" Jewell exclaimed. She rallied briskly, smiled through her tears, and stamped her feet in the snow. "I'd better get moving. My feet are freezing. Bye, Omar. It was nice seeing you."

Jewell dug her poles into the snow to start home, then turned around for a parting word. "I hope you appreciate your wonderful family and heritage."

She glided away, gradually fading into the shadows of shrubs and trees along a fencerow.

Omar turned toward home, no longer seeing the dazzling beauty of moonlit snow all around him. He was deep in thought.

16

Jealousy

As it turned out, that was the only real snowstorm of the winter. During January and February, the weather was mild with little snow and no ice for skating. A cold snap came during the last week in February, and the young people were hoping to be able to do some skating before winter was gone.

"The temperature's dropping," Joe reported enthusiastically, as he brought his pail into the cow stable to help milk.

"Good!" Mary responded happily. "I'm keeping

my fingers crossed for tonight." Annie Keim had sent word that the young people were invited to their skating party tonight if the weather held and the pond was frozen solid enough for skating.

"Okay, but how can you milk with your fingers crossed?" joked Joe.

"Just like this!" Mary squirted some milk right onto his face.

"Enough!" cried Joe. "Don't waste the milk."

For awhile, the only sound in the barn was the rhythmic swish-swish of milk streaming into the pails, and the contented sounds of the cows munching their grain. Then Mary broke the silence. "Say, Joe, what do you think of that Pete Byler from Summerville? He was at the singing on Sunday evening."

"Hmph! Not much!" Joe spat out the words. "He's so *grossfiehlich* (thinks he's so big)."

"But he's really good-looking, though," Mary countered. "And I heard Amelia say that he was a good friend of hers before she left Summerville."

"Good-looking, nothing!" Joe retorted. "He's a *Naaseweis* (smarty), turning up the rims of his hat and trying to look like a cowboy! The sooner he goes back to Summerville, the better."

"Well, I heard he's staying all summer and will be boarding at Franie J's place. So you might as well learn to like him."

"Rats!" muttered Joe darkly. He kicked at a hungry cat that came too close and sent her yelling, flying for cover.

"Why, Joe!" Mary was shocked. "Just what is wrong with you? That poor cat!"

Joe made no reply, but there was a big scowl on his face as he headed for the milkhouse with his pail of milk.

There must be more to this story than I know about, Mary mused as she poured her own bucket of milk through the strainer into the can. *I wonder why Joe's so touchy about Pete?* She filled a jug with milk and headed for the house.

"Brrr! It's cold," she said to herself, shivering. "But I'm glad. Skating party tonight!"

Susie held the door open for her. Her eyes sparkled. "We're having pancakes with maple syrup for breakfast. Nancy's making them."

"Mmmmm! You're making me hungry!" Mary gave Susie a quick hug.

Nancy stood at the stove, cheeks flushed from the heat, frying pancakes. "Good for you!" Mary encouraged her. "You know we all like pancakes and maple syrup."

The boys came trooping in from the barn, rosy-cheeked from the cold.

"Pancakes! I'm as hungry as three bears!" Henry exclaimed. "Nancy, please give me a teeny sample."

"No, you can wait," Mom declared. "Here, take these ashes out before breakfast is ready. Steven, you fill the coal bucket." She riddled the grate, took the ash pan out of the stove, and handed it to Henry. "Omar, will you get Lydia out of her crib? She must be awake because I heard her just a minute ago."

Omar went into the bedroom. Lydia, standing in her crib, held out her arms to him, smiling and prattling baby talk. "Oh, you little precious," he crooned, lifting her out of the crib. "You're so cute in those pink pajamas." He remembered what Jewell had said when he told her that he had a new baby sister: "You are so . . . so lucky." Well, she was right that time.

Dad and Joe came in from the barn, and the family was soon seated at the breakfast table. Dad opened the Bible to Matthew 5, and read.

> Blessed are those who hunger and thirst
>   after righteousness,
>   for they shall be filled.
> Blessed are the merciful,
>   for they shall obtain mercy.
> Blessed are the pure in heart,
>   for they shall see God.

Nancy sat listening, filled with quiet joy. She loved to hear her father read Scriptures in his deep, rich voice. It gave her a reverent feeling, knowing that "God's in his heaven—all's right with the world." She was happy with the glowing praise she received for what she had done all by herself, making pancakes with maple syrup, a rare treat for the family.

All day the weather cooperated beautifully for

Mary and Joe—clear, cold, and perfect for skating. Mary happily went about her work, eagerly looking forward to the evening.

Her happiness was dimmed a bit by Joe's sour mood, though, and she puzzled over it. Did Joe fear Pete as a possible rival? She pondered this while she was getting ready and decided to keep her eyes and ears open, to find out what she could. Perhaps she would even talk it over with Jacob.

The skaters, whirling and gliding on the smooth, ripple-free ice, made a pretty picture, and the air rang with the merry laughter and chatter of young people having fun.

Joe heard an especially hearty peal of masculine laughter mingling with Amelia's tinkling laugh, and he clenched his fists until his knuckles hurt. That Pete Byler again! What was he hanging around Amelia for? The nerve of him, flirting with someone else's girl.

Joe skated around the pond, edging nearer to where Amelia and Pete were. Should he barge in and claim his girl, asking her to skate with him? Or was he being too touchy? After all, Amelia and Pete were both from Summerville. Elmer and Ben came skating by, circling around and stopping in a shower of ice spray.

"Better watch out, Joe," Elmer teased. "If I were you, I'd hold onto that girl of yours. Look's like someone's trying to steal her away from you."

"Aw, cut it out," Joe drawled, trying to act unconcerned.

A fresh stab of jealousy pierced his heart when he saw that Pete and Amelia were skating together, hand in hand. Amelia was smiling that special smile of hers, the smile that he wanted her to reserve for him. He was struck by a feeling of hot anger, mingled with anxiety and fear, and an almost overwhelming desire to give Pete a shove that would send him flying across the ice.

At that moment Amelia turned around and called, "C'mon Joe, we're starting a game of crack the whip." She pulled her hand from Pete's, and skated toward Joe.

Fear left him, and a warm feeling wrapped his heart as she slipped her hand into his, and they skated off together.

"I want you to meet Pete Byler," she said, motioning to Pete. "He's been my good friend ever since school days."

"So this is the chap who stole Amelia away from me." Pete grinned good-naturedly and joked, "She was my childhood sweetheart." He winked at Amelia, and she giggled.

Joe's eyes narrowed. Was Pete only joking, or was he in earnest? If he was serious, he certainly didn't seem disturbed about it.

"Oh, shut up, Pete." Amelia was giggling again. "C'mon, let's go."

Crack the whip was lively and lots of fun. They all were breathless and panting when the party split up and they walked together to the buggy.

Amelia was her usual happy and talkative self on the way home, and Joe relaxed as his fears dissolved. No one would take Amelia away from him. Pete could go and bother the cat.

17

Beauty

It was springtime at Whispering Brook Farm. Nancy pushed up the window in her room and stuck her head out as far as she dared, drawing in great breaths of the fresh, sweet morning air. A turtle dove cooed softly from the spruce tree, and everywhere, it seemed, robins were joyously trilling and singing.

At the end of the lane, the weeping willow tree was covered with a pale yellow-green haze of new leaf growth. Nancy knew that in another month or so, her maple tree would again sprout new leaves,

and she could climb to her lofty hideaway without being seen. All the fields and dells and slopes of the entire farm were greening up, and in the hill pasture, Nancy could see the woolly new baby lambs with their mothers and hear their plaintive bleats. Last night she had heard the spring peepers for the first time. Jeremiah, the rooster, was crowing from the apple orchard.

The barn door opened, and Mary came out with a pail of strained milk, singing as she walked toward the house. Nancy put a screen in her window and busied herself cleaning her room. Springtime was for housecleaning, for airing winter clothes and putting them away.

Out in the barn, Dad was helping Omar harness the two big workhorses, Belle and Bo, for a day of spring plowing. Omar pushed open the wide rolling door, led the horses out, and backed them to the sulky plow.

Dad brought out two more workhorses to hitch up with Belle and Bo. "Remember, Omar," he said, "the horses aren't toughened up yet, so don't work them too hard. Let them rest often, and don't hurry them. And try to keep the furrows straight."

"Sure, Daed," Omar replied, taking the reins and climbing up on the seat. On such a lovely spring day, he was looking forward to plowing. Omar clucked to his four-horse team, and they were off, through the back lane, past the old apple orchard, heading for the west field.

At the edge of the field, he stopped the horses and lowered the plowshares. It gave him a feeling of satisfaction to see the rich black earth being turned over, with a neat furrow stretching behind him. He sniffed the air. It smelled of springtime and freshly turned earth, of woods and flowers and fields. Something stirred in Omar's veins, and he wanted to shout and dance and sing for joy. It was a good feeling. He thought of what Jewell had said: "I feel close to God. It's so beautiful."

As he topped a slight rise in the field, he could see Vaneski's house, a field's breadth away. Omar wondered what Jewell was doing. Secretly he hoped she was watching him—perhaps with binoculars—from one of the wide windows decorated with scrollwork.

At the end of the field, Omar let the horses rest for a minute while his mind wandered. He had not seen Jewell since the evening of the snowstorm, and ever since then he had been hankering to talk with her again. Sometimes he felt as if no one understood him. Jewell would understand, of that he felt sure.

He snapped the reins and started the horses on the next round. Omar hummed a tune as he imagined Jewell seeing him plowing, and coming out to the back end of the field to meet him, with an angelic smile on her sweet face. They would have a long talk, and then he would even let her ride on the plow, while he walked alongside, driving the horses.

She would love that. He could just see her clasping her hands in front of her, with rapture on her face.

Omar's daydreaming was interrupted by strange cries from the sky. He looked up, shading his eyes from the sun. Seagulls! The sky was filled with hundreds of gulls, dipping and sailing, following the plow, diving down for earthworms and grubs turned up by the plow.

The sun shone down warmer and warmer, the horses' flanks glistened with sweat, and their sides were heaving. Omar decided to let them rest longer than usual in the shade of an oak tree at the end of the field. He stretched his legs and looked at Jewell's house, daydreaming again.

It was so peaceful here. A breeze stirred the leaves, and the horses gently swished their tails. A groundhog's head popped up, about fifty feet away in the fencerow, and a moment later he cautiously climbed out, pulled several tufts of grass, took them into his den, and emerged again.

Omar's attention was drawn to Jewell's house again. A car was wending its way up the drive. It stopped, and a woman and a girl got out. The woman headed for the house, but the girl turned toward Omar and waved her arm in a wide arc. Omar's heartbeat quickened, and he waved back just as big.

Then she, too, disappeared into the house. Omar smiled as he clucked to the horses and turned them around. Jewell still remembered him! The thought warmed his heart and made him happy.

The forenoon passed quickly, and Omar was almost surprised when he heard the dinner bell ringing. As the horses plodded down the field lane, past the orchard, Nancy came running to meet him.

"*Mach schnell* (hurry), Omar," she called. "Charlie Kline's here with a new horse for you. He's just unloading him now."

Omar's eyes popped wide open when he saw the horse trailer parked beside the barn, just as Nancy had said. A horse for him! But he had been planning to tell Daed he didn't want one. He should have done it sooner.

Mixed feelings tumbled over each other as he watched Charlie lead out the beautiful shiny-black horse, looking up-headed and high-spirited. Omar quickly unhitched Belle and Bo and joined Dad and his brothers in admiring the new steed.

"Isn't he a beaut!" Joe whistled. "Say, Omar, what say you can have Chief, and I'll take this one?"

Omar merely shrugged his shoulders.

Dad was saying, "You're sure we can have him on trial for three weeks?"

"Yup," Charlie affirmed. "That's fair enough, I'd say. See ya later." He climbed in and drove off down the lane.

"But Daed," Omar began weakly, "I—I don't need a horse. . . ." His father gave him such a strange look that he quickly added, "Yet."

"But you'll be needing one by fall," Dad stated matter-of-factly. "This horse is only four years old and will need some training before then. He's broke, but a little green yet. Right after dinner, we'll hitch him to the two-wheeled training cart."

Joe led "Black Beauty," as Nancy dubbed him, around the barnyard several times.

"See how he arches his neck," Steven pointed out. "And how high he lifts his front feet."

"Yes, he has style all right," Dad agreed. "But that's not the most important part. He still has to prove himself on the road. Time will tell whether or not he's a sensible, decent horse. Put him away now, Joe. Let's go in for dinner."

Right after the meal, the boys went out to hitch up Beauty. Mary, Nancy, and Susie followed to watch.

"I just wish Omar would be as enthused about the new horse as Joe is," Dad confided to Mom, when they were alone. "I'm worried about him."

Mom nodded. "I've noticed, too, that he's not been himself since he came home from Amos and Bertha's. Maybe we should talk to him about it."

"It might be a good idea," Dad agreed. He went

out to help the boys hitch up Beauty and train him.

Grandpa came out on the porch to watch, leaning on his cane. Then he hobbled out the walk. From the window, Mom noticed with a pang how aged-looking and stooped he was becoming. *He's had a good long life,* she mused. *Nearly eighty-seven years.*

She lifted Lydia to the window. "See the pretty horsie," she said, pointing to Beauty. Now they had him hitched to the two-wheeled cart, and Dad and Joe got in.

"My, he's up-headed," Mom told Lydia. "And he wouldn't need to lift his feet so high."

Lydia squealed and clapped her hands.

As Beauty trotted out the lane, Lassie came bounding up from the meadow where she'd been sniffing out groundhog dens. Beauty stopped in his tracks, snorting and nervously eyeing Lassie.

"*Leicht nau* (easy now)!" Dad soothed him. "See, it's just a dog. Nothing to be afraid of."

As if able to understand what he was saying, Beauty calmly trotted on again.

"Yes, he's green," Dad commented, "but smart. He'll learn fast. Now we'll turn around and let Omar drive him."

18

Good-Bye

JOE and his two friends, Elmer and Ben, sat quietly on a bench in the living room at Cookie Dan's place, where Amelia boarded. The folding doors to the kitchen and bedrooms had been opened to make one large room, and benches had been set in neat rows for biweekly church service.

Joe shifted nervously on the bench. He knew that soon someone would announce the first hymn and began singing. At the beginning of the third line, the ministers would stand and go upstairs to a

room prepared for them. He and Elmer and Ben, and the five girls who had made application to join the church, would follow them for their first instruction class—while the congregation continued singing in a slow tempo.

Over the following eighteen weeks, there would be nine sessions of instructions in preparation for baptism. In each session, they would be reviewing articles of the 1632 Dordrecht Confession of Faith and rules of the church *Ordnung* (order). Then they would be baptized and received as members of the Amish church.

Finally the singing began, and soon the ministers arose on cue and filed upstairs. Joe felt self-conscious as he, Elmer, Ben, and the girls followed them. He knew all eyes were upon them, to see who was applying to join church. In the room upstairs, the young people sat on a bench facing the ministers. The bishop's voice was encouraging and sincere as he began to speak, and the applicants found themselves relaxing. They sat listening with bowed heads.

"It makes me glad to see that these young souls have expressed their wish to renounce the world and all sin, and to be baptized and accepted as members of the church," the bishop was saying. "This is the most important decision you will ever make. It is the most worthwhile step anyone can take—coming to Jesus in true repentance, and accepting him as Savior, and forsaking all sin, denying self, and keeping the ordinance of baptism."

The bishop's words were so earnest that Joe listened carefully. He went on, "It is very important that we are sincere. If we merely say with our mouths that we accept Jesus as our Lord, but then keep on living for ourselves and do not serve him, then it is meaningless. Baptism is only an outward symbol of a change that is wrought within the heart. But if we really are sincere, and come in true repentance to Jesus, God will accept us and give us the new birth."

The other ministers each spoke in turn, also instructing and admonishing. Joe felt a stirring in his heart, a longing to be true, worthy of a baptism that is not merely an outward ceremony. After the church services were over, the boys filed outside. Joe felt quiet and subdued. The ministers' words had impressed him, and he didn't feel like joining the other boys' light-hearted banter.

"Hey, Joe, you'd better walk the chalk line today," Ben whispered, poking him in the ribs. "Amelia's parents are here from Summerville."

Instantly Joe perked up. "Who? Where?" He had never met Amelia's parents, and he sure was interested. Joe had often wondered how Amelia's mom looked. Was she on the fancy side, too?

"See that woman talking to Cookie Dan's wife?" Ben had his hand over his mouth to direct his words to Joe alone. "That's her mom. And there's her dad, talking to Ben D. They drove up from Summerville

138

yesterday. You'd better behave yourself now!"

Joe glanced discreetly in the direction indicated, then walked on, satisfied. They were just ordinary Amish people and didn't look like "fence crowders" or seem to be out of the *Ordnung*. Amelia would grow up and settle down too, sooner or later.

Cookie Dan's family also hosted the singing that evening, and the young people were invited to stay for supper. Pete Byler was the life of the party and soon had everyone at the table, especially Amelia, laughing at his jokes. Everyone, that is, except Joe. He sat, unsmiling, resentment growing within him. *Why does that Naaseweis (smart aleck) have to come here and spoil everything?* he thought bitterly.

Joe was disappointed in Amelia, too. If she wasn't flirting, she came mighty close to it. Her laughter and chattering were an equal match for Pete's. Joe made up his mind then and there that he would say something to Amelia about it tonight. He shouldn't have to put up with this. But, as it turned out, Joe didn't have the chance. Immediately after the singing was over, Amelia sought him out. She said she had a terrific headache and was going straight to bed. There was nothing for Joe to do but go home.

His heart was heavy as he hitched up Chief and drove homeward. It was a beautiful spring evening, the spring peepers were singing, a silvery moon hung in the west, and the air smelled fresh and sweet. But the loveliness of the evening failed to cheer Joe. Somehow, he sensed that this was the beginning of the end of his relationship with Amelia.

Joe thought about how thoughts of Amelia and her parents had distracted him from the instruction class that morning. Maybe Daed had been right: perhaps it was better to wait for dating until one was baptized and a church member. As he drove in the lane at home, he saw Mary and Jacob going for a walk in the meadow. Loneliness filled his heart anew at the sight of their togetherness. He decided to get a good night's sleep. Maybe he would feel better by morning.

Sometime during the night, Joe awoke to hear it raining, and thunder was rumbling in the distance. Then he drifted off to sleep again.

The next morning dawned clear and bright after the rain. Everything was washed fresh and sparking clean, as if the sad old earth, by the rain's passionate tears, had been cleansed from filth and stain and had come forth radiantly pure and sparkling. Joe whistled as he hitched up Belle and Bo to the manure spreader. His spirits were lifting with the morning sun, and his muscles bulged as he forked load after load of manure into the spreader, then drove it out into the field.

The bits and pieces of manure flew out the back of the spreader, fertilized the fields, and "perfumed" the air. As he headed for the barn again, he squinted his eyes at the sunlight. Who was that coming up the lane in a trottin' buggy? A white-haired and white-bearded Amishman. A moment later he recognized him. Cookie Dan! What could he be wanting here? A stab of fear pierced Joe's heart. Did something happen to Amelia?

"Hello there," Dan called. "You're Joe, aren't you?"

Joe nodded. "Yes, that's right."

"Well, that's who I want to see. This morning I had to come past here to return something I borrowed at Ben D's, and when that hired girl of ours heard I was coming this way, she wrote a note to give to you." He reached into his pocket and drew out an envelope. "I don't know whether the tidings are for good or ill, and you won't find that out without reading it, so I'll be going on my way."

"Thanks," Joe groaned weakly, as Dan clucked to his horse and turned around. His knees were trembling as he ripped open the envelope. As he read, he realized his fears hadn't been groundless.

Dear Joe,
I will take this as my way of saying good-bye. This way, it's easier for me than saying it in person. I hope we can still be friends, even though nothing more. I wanted to tell you on Sunday evening already, but I didn't have the courage. I'm sorry.
Sincerely,
Amelia

Joe leaned against the barnyard fence. His face grew pale and rigid, and he broke out into a cold sweat. He clenched his hands at his sides, and a whirlpool of bitterness surged up inside. The beauty of the morning seemed to be a mockery to his misery now.

Sorry! What was she sorry about? Sorry that Pete had come up from Summerville? A feeling akin to hatred welled up within him at the thought of Pete. Joe knew this wasn't right, and as he struggled to overcome his anger, tears welled into his eyes.

He ripped the letter into tiny bits and tossed it into the back of the manure spreader. Then he picked up the pitchfork and set to work again. Perhaps hard work would help him to forget all about it.

19

Under the Pines

THE housecleaning was nearly finished—only the kitchen to do yet, and Mom and the girls were working at it. Mom was doing windows, Mary up on a ladder washing the ceiling, Nancy scrubbing the woodwork, and Susie polishing the stove.

"At least we have a beautiful day for this major undertaking," Mary noted, adding with a sigh, "although the great outdoors is simply beckoning me. Mamm, did you see how the bleeding heart bush is blooming, and the earth is just like a big smiling

greenness with a vast alluring blueness overhead?"

"I heard a bluebird singing," Nancy reported eagerly. "I do hope it builds a nest in the little birdhouse Henry put up."

From the toy box, baby Lydia came crawling over to Nancy's bucket of soapy water. She tried to pull herself up, but instead the bucket fell over, spilling a huge puddle of water on the floor.

"*Ach* (oh) my," Mom lamented. "Nancy, pick Lydia up quick, before she gets all wet." She went for a mop and began soaking up the water. "Why don't you and Susie take Lydia for a walk in the stroller? Mary and I can finish this. We only have the floor to do anymore."

When the little girls had left, Mary turned to Mom. "Mamm, did you notice that Joe hasn't been himself all week?"

Mom nodded. "Dad and I were wondering what's going on. What do you know about it?"

"Well, yesterday when I took a drink out to him in the field, I finally got it out of him. Amelia has quit him."

Mom sat down in the chair. "What happened?"

"I really don't know much, except that she has gotten pretty thick with Pete Byler from Summerville, since he's up here." Mary took the brush and began to work on the floor.

"Well, I think it'll work out for the best, even though Joe doesn't realize it now, and it likely wouldn't help to tell him that." Mom went back to washing windows. "I haven't heard many favorable reports about Amelia. Maybe by the end of the summer, when he's gone through all the instructions for baptism, he'll accept it better."

"It has gotten me to think, though." Mary was thoughtful as she scrubbed the floor mechanically. "How can I be sure . . . I mean, how can I know. . . ." She broke off in confusion, then began again, "How can I be sure Jacob is the right one for me, and that I'm really in love?" She blushed a shade pinker as she said it, hoping Mamm wouldn't laugh.

Mom pondered the question awhile, then replied, "True love isn't like they show it in romance books. It's not an overwhelming emotion that will hit you out of the blue—bang! It's something you grow into as you get to know your beau better. Love that lasts is built on character and ideals, not emotions.

"You might ask yourself some questions: Is he a genuine Christian? Is he kind-hearted and good-natured? Does he treat his horse well? Do you enjoy being with him? Is he sensible? Does he have a good character and lead a clean, faithful life? Do you respect and admire him? Would you want to spend the rest of your life with him?"

Mary laughed and relaxed. "I can certainly answer yes to all those questions about Jacob. I guess that means I'm in love, then." She quickly added, "It's not that I ever doubted Jacob, but it was a jolt for me to hear that Joe and Amelia broke up. I guess

I was a bit afraid that the same thing could still happen to us."

"I wouldn't worry about that," Mom consoled her. "I can tell that Jacob thinks a lot of you."

"Yes, I know," Mary admitted. "But Amelia also acted like she thought the world and everything of Joe. That is, until Pete came along."

"I know it's hard for him now," Mom stated, "but I think the day will come when he will be glad."

That Sunday there was no singing, so Jacob came early. It was another enchanting spring evening, and Mary suggested they could go for a walk in the fir grove. Robins were singing with joyous abandon in the maple tree, and the whistle of a cardinal could be heard from the pines.

"I see your garden things are up," Jacob remarked, as they strolled past. "You must've planted early."

"Yes, we did. But I keep thinking of last year's hailstorm, when all the early things were damaged by the hail."

"Well, that doesn't happen often," Jacob replied. Lassie came out of the barn and trotted along beside them. Jacob stroked her head. "Looks like you have a nice, intelligent dog, here. Is she a purebred?"

"Yes. We're planning to raise pups to sell."

"Good. I'd like to have one if I may. What's a farm without a dog?"

Mary raised her eyebrows and glanced at Jacob. "I thought you had a German shepherd at your place." Now they were walking in the grove, holding hands. The tall firs above them were quivering and sighing their mysterious tune.

Jacob smiled. "Did you hear that my dad bought a farm in Summerville?"

Mary stopped in her tracks. "No! For you?"

Jacob nodded. "*Fer dich aa* (for you, too), if you're willing." He was watching Mary closely for her reaction. She blushed and smiled, and Jacob knew that it was all right.

Half shyly, and half anxiously, he asked, "Do you think we could be married in November? We don't get possession of the farm right away, but by spring, I'll be doing the farming and—" He broke off in embarrassment, waiting for her answer.

"My answer is yes," Mary responded softly, lowering her eyes. "I'm sure it's all right with Mamm and Daed, too. They also were nineteen and twenty when they got married, so they can't say we're too young."

She faced Jacob with obvious joy. They sat down on the carpet of spicy, scented pine needles, and Lassie curled up at their feet.

"Tell me what the farm looks like," Mary said eagerly, ruffling Lassie's ear.

. Jacob chuckled. "One of the first things I noticed was that it has a little brook. Nancy would love that."

"So would I. And what's the house like?"

"Well, it's big, and it's old, like most of the farm-houses in Summerville, but it's in real good repair."

"Are there many trees on the property?" Mary asked anxiously. She was thinking, *I don't know if I could make myself at home if there were no trees.*

"Lots and lots of them," Jacob assured her. "In fact, if we'd do like Nancy did, we could name our land the Whispering Tree Farm or something like that."

Mary broke out with that infectious bubbling laugh of hers, dear to Jacob's ears. "A farm with trees and a brook! All this and heaven, too!" she murmured, smiling at Jacob, her eyes shining.

20

Cart Ride

WHEN Omar discovered that Black Beauty was an excellent riding horse, his feelings about him changed. Every chance he got, he threw the saddle on Beauty's back and rode off to the hills.

He loved the feeling of freedom and flying it gave him, and he enjoyed the beauties of springtime all around him in the fields and woods. Beauty liked to limber up, too, galloping across the fields, head tossed high, and mane flying in the wind.

On Saturday evening as Omar was saddling up

Beauty for a ride, Dad came out of the milk house.

"Well, Omar, how do you like your horse by now?" He stroked Beauty's glossy neck. "Are you pleased with him?"

"Oh, yes, Daed," Omar replied enthusiastically. "Someone certainly did a good job of training him for riding. It's no trouble at all to get him to canter."

Dad frowned slightly. "Omar, I wish you'd hitch Beauty to the cart a little oftener instead of riding him so much. After all, that's what he's for, to learn to be a good sensible road horse. We don't want him to canter and gallop when he's hitched to the buggy, you know." He caressed Beauty's silky mane as he spoke.

Omar hung his head and said nothing. He didn't want to hitch Beauty to the buggy and drive him that way. He could just hear Eph and Mony make fun of him. No, he'd much rather just keep on riding him. But how could he tell this to Dad so he would understand?

"Let's see, you'll be sixteen in September," Dad figured, counting the months. "If I'd order your new buggy now, it would be ready by fall when you'll be needing it. I heard that the coach makers are really busy, and you have to order nearly half a year in advance."

"No, Daed, don't order it yet," Omar replied quickly, almost guiltily. "I won't be needing a buggy that soon. I just want to ride Beauty," he added lamely.

"But you'll be needing a buggy when you start to *rumschpringe* (run around with the youth)," Dad sharply reminded him, with a note of fear in his voice. He wanted to shake Omar, to find out what really was wrong with him.

Omar swallowed hard. How could he tell Daed? There was no way he would understand. Words swirled through his mind: *self-righteous,* Heichler *(hypocrites), blame for arson.* No, he just didn't feel like joining the Amish youths yet.

Without a word, he stepped into the stirrup and swung himself up on Beauty's back. They were off to the hills without so much as a backward glance. Dad walked sadly to the barn with bowed head. Yes, sixteen was too young to start to *rumschpringe,* but when they didn't want to go, that was surely a thousand times worse.

Omar rode off to the west, toward a splendid golden sunset, but he hardly noticed it. His thoughts were in turmoil, and he needed some time to sort them out. Almost without realizing where he was going, he headed for the meadow woodland. Perhaps he would be able to think more clearly there, amid its elusive springtime beauty. Yet his musings were almost too deep for self-analysis.

A whippoorwill was calling, birds were singing everywhere, and the air was fresh and sweet. Beauty had walked into a patch of skunk cabbage, and the air became filled with pungent odor as his hoofs crushed it.

Suddenly Omar reined him in sharply. Just ahead, across the brook but still in the little valley, was a patch of lovely wild bluebells or hyacinths, and smack in the middle of it, sitting on a rock, was Jewell.

She had her eyes closed and was lifting her hands and face to the sky. There was a rapturous, angelic look on her face, almost as if she were receiving a benediction. Beauty snorted, and Jewell's eyes flew open in surprise.

"Omar!" she exclaimed, genuinely glad to see him. She gathered her bouquet of bluebells and came across the brook, stepping on stones so her feet wouldn't get wet.

"Oh, what a beautiful horse!" In delight she threw both arms around Beauty's neck, pressing her cheek against his. With slender, shapely hands, she threaded her bunch of bluebells into his bridle, then stood back to admire the effect. A smile played across her delicate face.

Omar watched, transfixed. Jewell was so enthralled by the horse that she had hardly noticed him yet. At last she turned to him. "You are so . . . so lucky . . . so blessed. You have everything . . . yes, everything." She sighed, and brushed away a tear.

At the sight of the teardrop, Omar's heart went out to her, but he also thought of himself. *She wouldn't say that if she knew about the turmoil in my heart.*

Jewell's eyes brightened again. "Would you . . .

do you think you could give me a ride sometime? I'd just love that."

Omar swiftly dismounted and handed Jewell the reins. "Sure, go ahead and ride Beauty. He's really well-mannered.

"No, no!" Jewell shook her head and backed away, clasping her hands behind her back. "I don't mean riding horseback. That's too bumpy. Could you hitch him to a buggy sometime and give me a ride? I never had a buggy ride."

"Okay," Omar agreed. "I'll ride back to the barn and hitch up. You wait at the end of your drive, and I'll pick you up there in a few minutes." He felt like he'd be willing to do anything for this sweet, friendly girl.

"Right now?" Jewell seemed amazed. "This is too wonderful." Ecstatic, she again clasped her hands in front of her. "Thank you, thank you!" she breathed. Then she started off briskly for home. "I'll be waiting for you at the end of the drive," she called back, in her lilting voice.

In a daze of happiness and excitement, Omar rode swiftly back to the barn. A few minutes later, Dad—from his chair inside the kitchen window, where he was reading the farm paper—was surprised to see Omar hurriedly throwing the harness on Beauty's back, hitching him to the two-wheeled cart, and driving out the lane at a fast clip.

"Beats me," Dad muttered to himself, shaking his head. "He must've changed his mind fast. I might as well order that buggy now, after all."

The mile's drive to Jewell's house was covered quickly. "I'm sure she doesn't know the difference between a buggy and a two-wheeled cart," Omar chuckled, as he spied the small figure waiting at her drive.

"Whoa, Beauty." He reined him to a stop. Jewell daintily stepped into the cart and seated herself. Omar, bursting with importance, clucked to Beauty, and they were off.

"Oh, Omar, this is great! I love it. I never had so much fun before in all my life. See how Beauty lifts his feet!" Her hair was streaming out behind her, blowing in the wind.

"Shall we go faster?" Omar asked. He loosened the reins, and Beauty picked up speed, his mane and tail blowing in the wind.

"No, this is fast enough for me," Jewell cried, clutching at Omar's arm. "I love it, though," she added, as Omar slowed the horse. "I feel like we're flying through that wonderful evening air. It's almost too beautiful for words."

The glory of the setting sun was fading, and Omar turned the horse around. "We'd better go back. Soon it'll be dark, and we don't have lights."

"Oh please, let's do this again sometime. Do you think we could?" Jewell turned imploring eyes on him. "I'd like nothing better."

"Sure," Omar replied, pleased at her obvious enjoyment of the ride. "I liked it, too."

He stopped Beauty at Jewell's drive again, and she hopped off. Once again she petted and caressed Beauty and crooned to him. Then she turned to Omar with a glowing face. "Thank you so much for the lovely ride. You're a wonderful driver! Such strong arms to hold back the horse. See you again soon."

Omar, blushing at Jewell's compliments, waved and nodded. He whistled a happy tune the rest of the way home. *You're a wonderful girl yourself, Jewell,* he thought. *And sweet and good, too.*

21

Unbroken Circle

It was apple blossom time, and the gnarled old apple trees in the orchard were laden with fragrant pink-and-white blossoms, indescribably beautiful, wondrously scenting the evening breezes over the entire farm. Nancy came into the kitchen with an armload of blossoms, raving about the enchantment of the orchard.

"It's so wondrously lovely, Mamm, we'll just have to take our supper out there," she proposed to Mom. "We worked hard enough today that we

earned a vacation, didn't we?"

Mom smiled at the impulsive enthusiasm of her daughter and gave her assent. "Yes, Nancy, you've certainly all done your part today, pulling weeds in the strawberry patch. Anyhow, I'd like to see the orchard myself. After all, blossom time only comes around once a year."

"Oh good, thank you, Mamm!" Nancy cried, giving her a quick hug. "You're the best mother in the world." She skipped over to her grandparents' end of the house to invite them. Then she flew outside to tell the rest of the family to do the chores before supper so they could have a leisurely picnic. The white lilac bush was blooming again, and Nancy stopped to breathe in great drafts of their sweet fragrance.

"It's such a lovely time of year," she murmured, scooping up one of Tabby's latest kittens. "How could anyone ever be happy living in the city? I feel so sorry for them."

Mary came out to the barn with her pail for milking. "You'd better carry lawn chairs up to the orchard for the old folks," she suggested. "They won't want to sit on the ground."

Nancy did as she was told. While the others were busy with evening chores, she helped her mother make sandwiches and salad, and they carried jugs of tea up to the picnic spot. Finally the day's work was done, and the whole family was assembled in the orchard.

"I'm glad it's a warm evening," Daadi said as he

hobbled to his chair. "If it were cool, I wouldn't be able to be out, on account of my rheumatism." Mammi helped him into a chair beside their son.

Dad was in good spirits because the corn planting was finished. To him, that in itself was reason for celebration.

Mom and Grandma sat visiting, while Mary and Nancy spread the big tablecloth on the ground and set out the food.

"Chow time," called Dad to the boys, who were pitching ball under the trees. They gathered around in a circle, all except little Lydia, who crawled into the center and began to help herself to a sandwich before the blessing had been asked.

Nancy sat back a little, basking in the goodwill of family togetherness times like these. *If only it could always stay like this,* she thought, for the hundredth time. *It's so beautiful.* The orchard was a great place for robins, and all around in the blossom-laden apple trees, they were singing cheerfully.

If this would be heaven, Nancy thought wistfully, *nothing would ever change, no one would leave to get married, no one would get sick or die.* She thought of the song, "Will the circle be unbroken by and by?"

Later the family was to think back on this evening as the cherished last time of family togetherness, with the unbroken circle, but no one suspected it then. The peace and beauty and loveliness of the spring evening surrounded them—the sublime, elusive magic of the blossoming trees, singing birds, and fragrant breezes.

Daadi was in one of his rare storytelling moods, and the others sat spellbound while he related to them stories of long ago. He told of the *gut aldi Daage* (good old days), when they brought the hay into the barn loose rather than baling it, when cattle and sheep were herded to market instead of being hauled on trucks.

During hard times, tramps roamed from farm to farm, asking for something to eat or permission to sleep in the barn. Then also, groups of gypsies asked if they could camp in the meadows; horse thieves and chicken thieves were common; and poor people came down from the mountains in horse-drawn carts, begging for food such as home-cured hams and bacon, produce, and hay for their horses.

Twilight came stealing over the old orchard, and a twinkling star appeared in the sky, then another. Baby Lydia fell asleep in Dad's arms, and Susie's head was nodding, too. But everyone was reluctant to move. Daadi was talking now, of his *rumschpringe* years, marriage to Mammi, and his first year of farming.

It's hard to think of Daadi as young and strong and muscular like Joe, Nancy mused. *And Mammi as a pretty young bride. And yet they say it doesn't seem so long ago.*

Joe sat listening to his grandpa's stories, and when the rest of the family had gone in, he remained sitting, deep in thought, with Lassie curled beside him. He wondered if Daadi had ever been quit by a girl, like Amelia had cut him off. In the weeks since, he had struggled against bitter feelings toward Pete and Amelia, and sometimes it seemed like a losing battle.

On Sunday evenings at the singings, when Pete drove up for Amelia and she stepped lightly into his buggy, Joe was almost surprised at his bitter feelings. He knew he should accept this as God's will, and forgive and forget. But it was the hardest thing he'd ever had to do.

He wondered if it would help him if he become interested in another girl. Arie Miller was nice. Although not tall and dashing like Amelia, she was pleasant and sweet-faced. Her eyes were dark brown and friendly, and there was a cute tilt to her nose. If she had a personality to match her looks, she would be all right.

Joe got up and stretched his arms to the sky. He muttered to himself as he planned: "I'll surely wait to ask her, though, until after I'm baptized, like Daed wanted me to." He walked toward the house, with Lassie following him.

22

Wounded Hearts

JUNE arrived, with all its beauty and charm. The rose arbor was covered with picture-perfect red roses, and their loveliness was surpassed only by their heavenly fragrance in the yard. Mary, Nancy, and Susie sat in the shade of the arbor, bowls in their laps, shelling peas.

It was a peaceful morning, and there was no indication of the unexpected drama that was about to unfold. Playful kittens frolicked in the grass, Jeremiah, the rooster, and his hens scratched in the

barnyard, and from the field came the clattering of the mowing machine, drawn by Belle and Bo, as Omar mowed the hay. The girls were admiring the beauty of the roses, and Mary was picking a few of the loveliest ones—when the kitchen door flew open and Mom hurried out.

"*Meed* (girls)!" she yelled, and there was alarm and fear in her voice. "Daadi has fallen and is unconscious! Mary, *dummel dich* (you hurry) to the phone shanty and call the doctor. Nancy, *schnell, schpringe* (quick, run) and tell Daed to come in."

Without a word, Mary dropped the roses—it was a long time before she could enjoy the sight of roses again—grabbed a scooter, and headed for the phone. Scootering was faster than walking, and just maybe . . . if she hurried fast enough, maybe the doctor could save him.

Instinctively, she knew it was bad. After all, Daadi was eighty-six years old, and he had a bad heart. With trembling hands, she dialed the doctor's number. What a relief to hear his calm voice, assuring her that he would be there as soon as possible.

Mary rushed back home to find the family, white-faced and frightened, gathered in Mami's kitchen. "How is he?" Mary asked Joe, in a whisper.

Joe shrugged. "Mamm and Daed are in the bedroom, trying to revive him. But I don't think they can do anything for him."

Finally they heard the doctor's car in the drive. He listened for Grandpa's pulse, peeked into his eyes, and looked for other signs of life. Then the children clearly heard him say, "He's gone. Likely death was fast and painless, coronary thrombosis, a blood clot in an artery. I expected that to be the case, because of his age and the condition of his heart. That's why I didn't send for an ambulance when you called."

Nancy threw herself into Mary's arm, weeping piteously. "It can't be," she cried. "We still need him!"

Mary stroked her hair. "Go ahead and cry," she murmured. She knew it was better to let grief out with tears than to bottle it up inside, with stony calm.

Joe went to the phone shanty, this time to call the relatives, or rather to have messages sent to them via *englisch* neighbors with phones. A short time later, relatives, friends, and neighbors began arriving in carriages, buggies, and on foot. Funeral arrangements had to be made. These kind folks, even with their presence, were showing concern, support, and willingness to help.

The family, especially Mammi, was in a daze, numb with the sorrow of parting with their loved one. In the following days, they were not expected to help get ready for the funeral. Others were at work everywhere, cleaning floors and windows and walls. The grass was cut, the peas picked and canned, and the laundry done. People came and went, offering assistance, bringing in meals, and helping with the chores.

Nancy had another outburst of sobbing when they brought Daadi's body back from the undertaker and they stood watching the coffin being carried into the house. Mary slipped an arm around her, comforting her, when they gazed on the peaceful, serene form on the white pillow.

"How will I be able to bear it when they put him into the ground?" Nancy whispered, with tears coursing down her cheeks.

"Just remember that it won't really be Daadi that they're burying," Mary reminded her. "That's just the body or house he lived in while on earth. The real part of him is with Jesus, and like unto the angels."

At bedtime, Mary could not sleep, even though she was worn out with the day's pain and excitement. She knelt by the window in the darkness and prayed, looking up to the stars above the fir grove. The night was warm and tranquil, and the house was hushed, almost as if angels were hovering above it to transport Daadi's soul to heaven.

Mary thought of the coffin in the parlor, where dear old Daadi's body lay. His sparse gray hair framed his peaceful face, which they would see no more on this earth after the funeral. She had not yet shed even one tear, but now she allowed them to flow freely, and afterward she felt cleansed and peaceful. She knew it was God's plan that earthly life should have its limits, but the parting was hard, especially so for Mammi.

"*O himmlische Vadder* (heavenly Father)," Mary

whispered, "help Mammi to be able to bear it. Support us all through the times of loneliness for Daadi. Heal our wounded hearts, and comfort and strengthen us all. Amen."

Funeral services were held in the Petersheim home, with all the folding doors opened wide to make one big room on the first floor, like they would for regular church services. Everyone dressed in black.

Seated in rows on benches, they listened as the minister read aloud a hymn. He then spoke about the glorious hope of the resurrection for believers, eternal life, and the joy of meeting the beloved departed one again someday, on that beautiful shore.

"Death is the door to life for God's children," the minister said softly but earnestly. Then, changing his approach, he spoke words of warning to those who had not yet given their hearts and lives to the Lord and were still living in sinful, selfish desires. "Life is uncertain," he went on, "and not everyone has until age eighty-six to prepare to meet God."

After the services were over, they filed past the coffin for one last look at the departed. The people were solemn and hushed. Then the hostlers led the horses and carriages to the front walk. One by one, the families of Daadi's children got in. In a long procession, they followed the horse-drawn hearse to the graveyard.

Mom, Dad, Grandma, and the three youngest girls were in the first carriage behind the hearse. Next were the uncles and aunts. Then Joe, Omar, Mary, Steven, and Henry rode in the two-seated carriage drawn by Chief, and behind them was a long string of buggies and surreys, wending their way to the graveyard to watch the burial.

"This is the last time Daadi will be traveling this road," Joe remarked somberly. "He lived here on this farm all his life, and I wonder how many times he went this way in his nearly eighty-seven years."

"Yes, Daadi's going away for the last time," Mary mused. "Away from the fields he tilled for many years, the trees he planted, the orchard he tended. I doubt that there are many people who live on the same farm all of their life, without living anywhere else."

At the graveyard, the pallbearers removed the coffin from the hearse and carried it to the newly dug grave. As the clods were shoveled on top, words came to Mary's mind: "Dust thou art, to dust returnest, Was not spoken of the soul." *His soul is with God,* she reminded herself. *And he had a good long life here on earth.*

A song sparrow sang from a tree nearby, and a gentle breeze rippled the grass. To Mary, that was a token of God's love and of his promises. "Truly God does all things well," she murmured. "God's in his heaven—all's right with the world."

23

Honeysuckles

OMAR had been quiet and withdrawn since
Grandpa's passing. He hadn't much heart for anything. To him, death was mysterious and incredible.
He imagined he saw Gramp everywhere, yet found
him nowhere, that stooped kindly figure, leaning on
his cane. Omar's heart ached with loneliness and a
sense of loss.

Jewell had sent him a sympathy card, which he
carefully tucked away in his bureau drawer. She had
signed it, "Luv you, Jewell." He took the card out of

his drawer and looked at it again. Did she really love him? Suddenly he had a strong desire to see her again.

He rushed downstairs and out to the barn to harness Beauty and hitch him to the two-wheeled cart. It was rather late, but perhaps Jewell was out for a stroll, anyway.

Beauty had not been driven for nearly a week and was feeling frisky and full of pep. At the entrance to Vaneski's drive, Omar stopped and waited, hoping Jewell would see him and come running. But she was not in sight, and Beauty didn't want to stand. On a sudden impulse, feeling daring, he turned Beauty into the drive. Omar drove on up to the house, turned around, then stopped at the front gate. A moment later the door was flung open, and Jewell ran out and hopped into the cart beside Omar.

"I was praying you would come for me," she confessed, half shyly. "I'm so glad. I just love going for drives with you. Oh, doesn't that fresh air smell heavenly? What is it, anyway?"

"It's probably honeysuckles," Omar told her. "Down along the road banks, there's some growing on both sides of the road."

"Oh, let's stop," Jewell trilled. "I never knew honeysuckles smelled so sweet." Hopping down, she pulled off a few of the vines and twined them into Beauty's mane. "Driving with a horse is so much nicer than in a car," she exclaimed. "When we passed that place with the car, I never even noticed any honeysuckles growing there, much less smelling them. In a car, you just whiz past, with no time to enjoy the scenery."

"How about in the winter, though? Don't you think you'd freeze?" Omar teased, with a grin.

Jewell wrinkled her pretty little nose. "If you people can stand it, I could, too," she declared staunchly. "I'm not a cream puff."

Omar glanced quickly at Jewell. Was there a hidden meaning in her word? But she was looking at the wildflowers along the road bank, and her face was innocent of expression. Soft brown curls framed her face, and she was wearing a lacy, ruffled blouse.

"I was sorry to hear about your grandfather." Her tone was sympathetic as she turned to Omar. "You must miss him a lot."

Omar nodded. It was still almost too painful for him to talk about it, even to Jewell. Sensing this, Jewell added, "Just remember how happy he must be, though. I've often thought about what a beautiful place heaven must be. Oh! What road is this? How quaint! How lovely!"

"It's just a field lane through the woods," Omar told her. "Actually, it's a short cut to Covered Bridge Road."

"Could we go that way?" Jewell implored. "I'd just love that!"

Omar hesitated. If they went that way, he'd have to pass Whispering Brook Farm to take Jewell home.

What if someone would see them?

"Could we, please?" She clasped her hands. "It looks so dear and interesting."

Omar pulled on the left line, guiding Beauty onto the dirt road. Here the banks on either side were covered with wild roses and tangled honeysuckle vines in profusion. The track was arched over with huge, wide-spreading trees, and a rose-colored sunset sky shone through the boughs.

"Oh, this is indescribably beautiful!" Jewell exclaimed, lifting her radiant face to the splendor all around them. "It's heavenly." She sat spellbound and dreamy eyed, taking deep breaths of fragrant evening air. The dirt road was a mile long, and Jewell sat entranced, enjoying every minute of the ride.

Omar was watching her expression as her emotions played across her sensitive face.

Suddenly Jewell snapped to attention. "What's that?" she gasped. "A little graveyard! Omar, it is really? We've just got to stop."

"Yes, that's what it is. Whoa, Beauty." Omar drove up to the fence surrounding the graveyard and tied Beauty to it. "We'll have a little time to explore it before sundown."

The grass grew thick and long around the old sandstone slabs, but most of the writing on them was still visible.

"Here's one with a date of 1789," Jewell pointed out. "My, that's old." There was a touch of awe in her voice. "There's something almost sacred or hallowed about being in a graveyard, isn't there?" she murmured. "These people who have lived and loved and toiled, probably right here in this neighborhood, lying beneath us, under the sod . . ." Her voice trailed off.

"See what it says on here, Omar." She pointed to a small, low gray stone. "To My Dear Beth, and Our Little Son," Jewell read aloud. "I imagine that must have been a young mother who died in childbirth. How hard that would have been for the young husband, losing both his wife and son." She brushed a tear from her cheek.

"Listen to this verse." Omar read it aloud in a solemn voice.

My cheeks were rosy; my countenance fair.
No one knew that death was near.
So prepare, dear friends, live each day for God.
Your body, too, will rest beneath the sod.

"That's hard to realize, when one is young and healthy, full of life and energy." Jewell was pensive. "But it's very true, a reminder that 'life is real! Life is earnest!' Eventually, death is sure to come."

Omar nodded in agreement. He marveled at Jewell's insight and wisdom. She was so different from the town girls who had come out to the farm to pick strawberries. They were silly, always giggling and chattering nonsense. Jewell was sweet and good, and he wondered at the difference.

As the sun was setting behind the wooded hill, Omar briskly declared, "I'm afraid we'll have to be going if we want to be off the road by dark. I don't have lights on this rig. Maybe we can come back again some other time."

They hopped into the cart and in a few minutes were on the Covered Bridge Road. Omar let Beauty have free rein, and his feet fairly skimmed over the road.

"This feels like flying." Jewell laughed. Her hair was flowing, and Beauty's mane was flying in the pleasantly cool evening breeze.

Soon they were passing Whispering Brook Farm, and Omar hoped it was dusk enough that no one would see them. But on the other side of the lane, they met Joe on the scooter, probably coming home from the phone shanty. His eyes widened in surprise when he saw them. He managed to return Jewell's wave, but stared after them in amazement.

"That was Joe, wasn't it?" Jewell asked. "He's almost as good-looking as you are."

Omar momentarily forgot his irritation at having been seen by Joe. He smiled at Jewell's compliment, and when he dropped her off at her home, she gave him another one.

"I appreciate you so much, Omar," she remarked warmly. "You're a real gentleman. Can we go for a drive again soon?"

"How about Wednesday evening?" Omar's face flushed with warm feelings. "I'll pick you up here, again, if that's all right."

"That's fine! I'll see you then." There was a lilt to Jewell's voice. "Good night!"

Omar whistled a happy tune as he drove home, put Beauty into the barn, and slipped up the back stairs to his room. He didn't want to meet anyone just now. Life was happy and interesting again.

24

Healing

THE Petersheim family discovered that life goes on after a death in the family. In the days following the funeral, Nancy found that tears were often near the surface. She had spent a lot of time with her grandparents and was close to them.

Now she missed Daadi terribly. Her parents gave her permission to sleep at Mammi's end of the house. It soothed Nancy to be near her, and it was a comfort to Mammi, too, to have her granddaughter there.

In the night after the funeral, Nancy awakened. With the stillness and darkness all around, her sorrow came flooding back. She remembered how Daadi had taken her side and kindly put up the Whispering Brook Farm sign for her.

Nancy had asked Daadi if he thought it was dumb, making a sign like that, and she had loved his answer: No, indeed, I thought it was clever. The memory of it brought tears to her eyes, and she shook with sobs. The door to Mammi's room was open, and when she heard the sobs, she went over to comfort Nancy.

"It's all right to cry." Grandma knelt down and put an arm around the grieving girl on the bed.

"Oh, Mammi, I can't bear it. I miss Daadi so," sobbed Nancy. "I wish he'd still be here."

"I miss him, too." Grandma brushed away a tear of her own. "But I keep reminding myself that he's in a better place. I would not wish him back. I would rather go to him."

"Things will never be the same again, Mammi. And yet we have to go on living. But how can we?"

"Nancy dear, we'll only have to live one day at a time. And Jesus has promised to be with us every step of the way. Remember that he said, 'I will never leave you nor forsake you.' "

Nancy nodded in the darkness. "Stay with me, Mammi, the rest of this night," she begged in a small voice. "It's not lonely when you're here."

❖ ❖ ❖

Gradually, affairs slipped into their usual routine at Whispering Brook Farm. Work was done and duties fulfilled with regularity as before, although not without aching pangs of loss at times. The raspberries were ripe. Although the Petersheims didn't have as many of them as strawberries, they still spent long hours in the raspberry patch, plucking the "purple jewels," as Nancy called them, and packing them to be sent to local grocery stores. On Monday morning Nancy and Mamm were picking side by side, while Susie and Lydia played in the sandbox in the yard.

"You know, Mamm," Nancy reflected, "it makes me feel almost sad that things go on like usual without Daadi. This morning Lassie was jumping up in the air, trying to catch a flea, and I laughed out loud. It made me feel guilty to laugh. I feel as if I shouldn't be happy, with Daadi not here."

"Do you think Daadi would want you to keep on being unhappy and mourning for him?" Mom asked gently. "He'd want you to find pleasure in the pleasant things around you, and in the companionship of other people." She paused, listening to the cheerful singing chirping of the purple martins as they circled around their martin house, feeding their young.

"I don't think we should shut our hearts to the healing that God gives to us," she continued. "But I know how you feel. We seem disloyal when the one we love is no longer here to share the happiness—almost unfaithful to our sorrow."

Nancy pondered this a few moments. "At first I couldn't bear to think of Daadi. . . . It hurt me to think of him. But now . . . it's a comfort to me. I'm glad I have lots of memories of him. Mamm, do you think it would be all right for me to take down that Whispering Brook Farm sign? I'd like to put it away in a safe place. Some cherished memories of Daadi go with it, and I'd just rather . . . ah . . . not have it up on the barn anymore," she finished lamely.

Mom chuckled. Nancy sure was full of strange ideas sometimes. "Go ahead and take it down. Mary was after me to get one of the boys to take it down before her wedding, anyway. She'll be glad if you do."

"*Was* (what)!" Nancy exclaimed. "Mary's *Hochzich* (wedding)? You mean she's thinking of getting married *schunn* (already)?" Her voice was full of shock.

Mom nodded. "But don't tell the younger ones. We'll have to keep it a secret until she's published. And the wedding won't be till November."

Susie came out to the raspberry patch, leading Lydia by the hand and bursting with importance. "Mary told me a secret," she bubbled happily. "It's a surprise for you. I can hardly wait! I'm going to set the table for Mary, then when you come in, you'll see it." She skipped back to the house.

Nancy picked up Lydia. She was chubby and cute, learning to lisp a few words. Just last week

Mom had started to put up her hair in *bobbies* (banded loops of hair), which made her cuter than ever.

"Oh, you little *Liebschdi* (sweetheart)," Nancy crooned, kissing her on the cheek. Lydia wrapped her arms around Nancy's neck. "You're sweet, but you do need another diaper." Nancy carried her out of the raspberry patch and then walked her through the yard toward the house.

The dinner bell was ringing, and Dad and the boys came in from the field. The first thing everyone saw when they entered the kitchen, was the platter of steaming ears of corn on the cob.

"Whoopee!" Henry shouted. "*Rooschtniers* (roasting ears)!"

"My, sweet corn already!" Dad marveled. "We've never had any this early before. What kind is it?"

"It's new," Mom answered. "Super Early Gold. I hope it tastes as good as it looks."

Nancy felt a stab of guilt as she took the first luscious bite of sweet corn. She remembered how, at first, after Daadi had died, she thought she would never be hungry again or enjoy good food. But then she recalled her talk with Mamm. Smiling, she sank her teeth into the corn on the cob. It was all right. Life was good.

25

Promises to Keep

SUMMER passed on work-laden wings. The women-folk were busy canning. They put up lots of extra jars of fruits and vegetables, for Mary and Jacob would be housekeeping before another canning season came around. The boys painted the barn and chicken house. Everything had to be shipshape for the wedding.

Dad, with the boys' help, enclosed the back porch to make room for the wedding tables. Along one wall he put a formica-topped counter with slid-

ing doors, and at the other end, built-in corner cupboards.

It's beautiful," Mary sighed. She wished time would go faster, yet there was still so much to be done that she sometimes feared they wouldn't be ready by November.

Joe found it easier to concentrate at the biweekly instruction meetings without Amelia to distract him. He found himself looking forward to those Sunday sessions. Sometimes he felt that giving up his self-will was getting easier, and at other times, it seemed like a losing battle. He wanted to deny selfishness and give Christ first place in his life, on the path to Christian manhood. But he knew he could not do it in his own strength. He was eager to learn more and become familiar with the eighteen articles of faith.

Joe tried to push any thoughts of Amelia and Pete to the back of his mind, but he was not always successful. Sometimes when he heard her tinkling laugh at the Sunday evening singings, a bitterness welled up inside. It was not for him anymore; now it seemed to mock him. His thoughts turned more and more to Arie Miller.

Whenever he saw Arie's sweet, gentle face, with those brown eyes and dimpled cheeks, his heartbeat quickened. He hoped no one else would ask her before he was able to, after his baptism. Sometimes he wondered if she felt his gaze upon her, or whether she was completely unaware of his interest in her.

In two weeks Joe would be a church member.

Then he would be free to ask Arie for a date. Would she think enough of him to accept?

The September Sunday of the baptismal services dawned clear and bright. It was one of those brisk autumn days when a person feels overwhelmed by the beauty of nature and wants to spend as much time outdoors as possible, drinking in the fresh fall air and all the breathtaking scenery.

That Sunday, church services were at Ben D's. Elmer, Ben, and Joe sat together on a bench, waiting for the first hymn to be announced. Today would be their last instruction meeting with the ministers, to receive private counsel and admonition. Finally the hymn was announced, and men's and women's voices, singing in unison, filled the house.

On the third line, the ministers got up and led the way to an upstairs room, followed by the class of applicants. The topic this time was the seventeenth and eighteenth articles of faith, on the *Meiding* (shunning the separated), and on the resurrection of the dead and the last judgment.

The bishop wrapped up the sessions with some general advice and instructions. He reminded them to dress plainly, according to the *Ordnung* (rules) of the church; to abstain from worldly amusements, drinking, and carousing; not to yield to lusts of the flesh; and to live faithfully according to the Scriptures.

"Let all your actions be according to the golden rule, and let your conduct be kind and gentle," he went on. "Return good for evil. Be truthful, and let your light shine before the world, so that they may see your good works, and glorify your heavenly Father."

The young people felt the earnestness in the bishop's voice and the solemn gravity of the step they were about to take. Today was the day they would promise, on bended knees, to be faithful to God and the church. They were dismissed to go downstairs and sit just behind the ministers' bench. After the *Aafang* (opening sermon), the congregation knelt for prayer. Then the deacon got up and read the text, a chapter chosen from the New Testament.

A visiting minister had the main sermon, expounding truths from the text and speaking about the duties of young people entering the Christian life. He called on them to walk the straight and narrow way even through difficulties.

After other ordained leaders affirmed the message, everyone knelt again for prayer. The bishop prayed aloud for the young souls about to make lifelong promises and asked God to strengthen every member to make good on their own baptismal pledges.

Then the deacon went out and returned with a pitcher of water for observing baptism. The applicants knelt before the bishop, and he asked them,

"Are you willing, with the help of God, to renounce the world, the flesh, and the devil, and to be obedient only to God and his church?"

In turn, each answered, "Yes."

"Do you promise to walk with Christ and his church and to remain faithful through life and until death?"

Each promised, "Yes."

"Do you confess that Jesus Christ is the Son of God?"

Each candidate affirmed, "I believe that Jesus Christ is the Son of God."

With the rest of the congregation standing, the bishop prayed for those to be baptized and asked for God's blessings upon their lives. Then the bishop stepped up to Joe and held loosely cupped hands above his head. The deacon poured water through his hands three times, while the bishop solemnly declared, "I baptize you in the name of the Father, and the Son, and the Holy Spirit."

After baptizing all the applicants, the bishop took Joe by the hand and said, "In the name of the Lord and the church, I extend my hand. Stand up and be counted as a faithful brother of the church." The bishop greeted Joe with a holy kiss. He repeated the same with Elmer and Ben. Then he welcomed the young women as sisters in the church, and the bishop's wife greeted them with a holy kiss.

It was a cleansing, soul-satisfying experience for Joe, and in the following week his thoughts often returned to it. He wanted, with God's help, to remain true to his baptism, to continue to renounce sin, and to be a light to the world, as the bishop had said.

Now he could begin to date Arie—if she was willing.

26

The Chill

AROUND Whispering Brook Farm was a pleasant stir of excitement that deepened as the days went by. Preparation for the wedding was beginning in earnest, but no one outside of the family was to know it yet, not until Mary and Jacob were published at church.

Every room in the house was freshly repainted or papered, new linoleum was laid in the kitchen, and an addition was built to the washhouse. Joe and Arie were going steady now. Joe was to be a witness

on Mary's side, and Jacob's cousin Anna Fisher was to be the other witness. He wished that Arie could be a witness with him, but at least she would sit next to him at the supper table.

Arie was a girl of high standards, and Joe found that dating her was quite different from dating Amelia. There was depth and sincerity in Arie's character that he had never seen in Amelia. She was not the dashing, flippant, outgoing type like Amelia, but there was an air of wholesomeness about her. Sometimes Joe had the feeling that he was unworthy of such a girl.

Omar's new buggy had arrived, and one evening he hitched Beauty to it for the first time. He felt happy and excited. It was shiny and new, and now he could take Jewell for rides in style, instead of on the bumpy two-wheeled cart. His heart sang as he drove up to Jewell's house. The trees were changing color, hanging out lovely shades of red, gold, and brown, and there was an invigorating crispness in the air. The silo had been filled, and the fields were bare again, giving open space back to the countryside.

When Jewell came out and climbed into the buggy, she did not have her usual bouncy verve. She seemed troubled about something and barely noticed the shiny new buggy.

"What's wrong?" Omar asked anxiously, feeling let down.

"We need to talk. Could we go up that lovely woods road again, where the graveyard is? It's so quiet and peaceful there."

"Sure." He headed Beauty in that direction, and soon they were driving along under the lovely arched trees. Goldenrod was still blooming in the fields, and fragrant wild grapes dangled from the vines and perfumed the air.

"Oh, it's so lovely here," Jewell breathed. "How can I bear to leave it all?"

"Leave?" Omar echoed. "What do you mean? Are you moving?"

Jewell nodded, tears blinding her eyes. "We're going back to California for the winter. We'll return next spring, though, but I'm going to miss you terribly. Your friendship has meant so much to me." She was crying now, her shoulders shaking, and her hair falling over her face.

Omar's shoulders slumped. So she was going. What if he never saw her again? He had nourished a wild dream that one day she might be his, but now that hope was draining away.

"I really don't blame you for not wanting to join the Amish," Omar confided bitterly. "You probably noticed that most of them are either self-righteous or hypocrites."

Jewell's head jerked up. "What do you mean?" she asked sharply. "I haven't noticed anything of the sort."

Suddenly Omar found himself telling Jewell everything about Henner Crist's twins and their attitudes. He shared how they had influenced his view of the other Amish, and how he was blamed for arson. It relieved him to be telling her everything, to be unburdening these bad feelings to someone.

When she spoke again, Jewell was incredulous. "You mean you let those two bad boys influence you like that? Do you really think the Amish people are only pretending to be righteous, or are haughty and proud of their righteousness?"

When Omar didn't answer, she asked again, "Do you really?"

Omar shrugged uncomfortably. When she put it that way, it made him look ridiculous.

Jewell's voice softened. "I have deep respect for the Amish people. I admire you all so much. Of course, there may be a few self-righteous or hypocrites among you, but why judge all by those few?"

Beauty had stopped of his own accord and was eating grass beside the dirt road.

"I'd love to join the Amish," Jewell went on, "but something deep down tells me I'd never fit in."

Omar started to protest, but she didn't wait.

"I've decided to go to college and then to medical school to become an obstetrician." She said it quietly, with a catch in her voice.

"Don't you care for me at all?" Omar was downcast, and his last bit of hope was quickly evaporating.

"Oh, I do care a lot for you!" Jewell burst out passionately. "The thought of doing without your friendship is almost unbearable to me. But . . . well,

I guess I don't care for you the way you have in mind. I'm so sorry. I never realized I was leading you on. I never once thought you'd take it that way.

"It's all my fault," she sobbed. "I was lonely, and I dearly loved going for drives with you. Forgive me, please!"

Omar picked up the reins and clucked to Beauty. It was gloomy under the trees, so he snapped on the buggy lights. "There's nothing to forgive," he assured her. "You haven't been leading me on." He was angry at himself for having imagined romance into the friendship.

"This was the happiest summer I ever had." Jewell was smiling through her tears. "Will you take me for drives again next summer?"

When Omar didn't answer right away, she begged, "Pretty please?"

In spite of his disappointment, Omar had to laugh. "Sure, if you still want to then."

"Oh, I'm sure I'll want to. Take good care of Beauty till then."

Now they were at her house. Jewell got off and patted Beauty on the neck. She blew a kiss to Omar, then turned and walked away, tears streaming down her face.

Omar waved farewell and quickly turned his face aside so she would not see his own tears.

On the way home, he let Beauty have free rein and was not aware of the chill in the night breeze.

27

Qualms

THE week before the wedding, Nancy came home from school with a tragic face, threw her books on the table, and burst into tears.

"*Was ewwer is letz* (whatever is the matter)?" Mom asked, alarmed. "Aren't you feeling well?"

"Oh, Mamm, my head's awful *beissich* (itchy)," Steven complained, scratching his head. "I know what's wrong with Nancy, too."

"Lice!" Henry cried, holding his cap at arm's length. "The whole school has them."

Mary sat down hard in a chair and covered her face with her hands. "Just when we're so busy getting ready for the wedding, now all this extra work," she wailed. "It can't be true."

But it was true. Joe was dispatched to the drugstore for Quell shampoo and Rid spray. School was closed for two days, and no one was allowed to come back until they were rid of the loathsome critters. All heads were shampooed with Quell, then combed with a fine-toothed comb. Bedding was washed, caps and coats sprayed with Rid.

Mom and Mary worked until midnight, washing and scrubbing everything that might possibly have come into contact with the lice or their nits. It seemed like a nightmare, but finally it was over, and Mary sank wearily into bed, every bone in her body aching. Time would tell whether or not they had gotten them all. If not, and someone was reinfested, they'd have to go through all that work again.

Mary told Jacob all about it on Sunday evening as they wandered down to the brook after the singing.

"That reminds me of the time our school had them, when I was in the eighth grade," he said, chuckling. "My older sister thought it was such a disgrace, but Mom told her it's not a disgrace to get lice, only to keep them."

"Well, it sure isn't a pleasant thing, especially when we're getting ready for a wedding."

Jacob was sympathetic. "Are others giving you enough help to prepare for the wedding?"

193

"Yes. Most of the cleaning is already finished, and on Wednesday the uncles and aunts are coming to butcher the turkeys and chickens and bake the bread, pies, and cakes. I can hardly believe it's only four more days till we're married!"

"I was up at our farm in Summerville last week," Jacob told her. "I wish we could move there right after the wedding."

"I know," Mary agreed. "But that would never do. Right after our *Hochzich* (wedding), we have to do our visiting, over the winter, and wait until spring to move."

Jacob nodded. "I guess we'll have to do it that way, since it's the custom. We'll each keep living with our parents, but at least we'll be together every weekend, and oftener over the wedding season."

"I hope this nice *Altweiwersummer* (Indian summer) weather holds," commented Mary. "Wouldn't it be nice to get married out here by the brook, with the golden leaves floating down, and the blue sky overhead?"

Jacob chuckled. "I can tell that you're Nancy's sister. That sounds more like one of her ideas. By the way, why do you think she took down that Whispering Brook Farm sign?"

"I think it was because cherished memories of Daadi were connected to it. She wanted to put it away for safekeeping. Nancy seems to miss Daadi the most, and she took his death the hardest, too."

"How will she take it when you leave home? She

finds it hard to adjust to changes, doesn't she?"

"Yes, she does, but I guess she'll just have to accept it. I'm more worried about how *I'll* be able to adjust to marriage. Sometimes I have a feeling of being in a dream, walking along, drawn like a magnet toward a drop-off. Then I wonder what will happen to me when I step off firm, familiar ground, into the unknown."

"Don't worry, you won't fall," Jacob teased. "I'll catch you, and we'll live together happily *immer derno* (ever after)."

Their laughter mingled with the sound of water gurgling over stones in the brook.

Then, more seriously, he asked, "You're not wishing you wouldn't be taking the step, are you? Don't you feel ready for it yet?" There was an anxious look on his face.

Mary put his fears at rest with that infectious, bubbling laugh of hers. Then softly she declared herself again. "I'm ready to go with you to the ends of the earth, if necessary. I love you, Jacob. But I suppose every girl has some qualms about stepping out of young maidenhood, into the role of being a wife, don't you think?"

Jacob nodded. "I guess I'll have to admit I'm having some qualms myself. What if I won't be able to make you happy? What if you'll get dreadfully homesick so far away from your family, and beg to go back to your mother?"

Mary giggled. "I'm not the least bit worried

about that. I'm happy when I'm with you, and I can hardly wait to start housekeeping and having a home of our own. I guess it was mostly my own weaknesses and shortcomings I was worried about, wondering if I'd be able to be a good wife for you, and all that."

Jacob looked at his bride-to-be with shining eyes. "If that's all you were worried about, you can quit right now. You're my ideal of all that's beautiful and good, Mary."

Mary blushed and lowered her eyes.

"I think if we can keep Christ as the head of our home," Jacob continued huskily, "he will help us to be kind and considerate of each other's feelings, and forgiving of each other's faults. God will bless our marriage with happiness and love."

Mary nodded, her heart too full for words. They sauntered back to the house in the twilight and visited a bit with the family. Then Mary held King while Jacob hitched him to the buggy. "I'll come tomorrow to help get ready for the wedding," he told her. "Good-bye till then."

Mary stood watching the buggy lights recede into the darkness. Her thoughts traveled back to their first date, the time the midwife's car had been parked in the lane. Yes, theirs was a happy courtship. Now it was leading to marriage, and their *rumschpringe* years were over. But Mary wasn't sorry. She looked forward, with eager anticipation, to her new role in life.

28

Wedding Day

MARY wakened early on the morning of her wedding day and peered anxiously out the window to check the weather. The stars were still twinkling in the sky, and it looked to be the dawn of a beautiful day. She happily dressed and hurried downstairs. There were so many last-minute things to be done.

The house was spotless, and the benches were set in place, but chores must be done, breakfast eaten, and dishes washed. The little girls must be combed and dressed in their new dresses, aprons, and head coverings.

The cooks came early to roast turkeys and chickens, prepare the dressing, peel the potatoes, and make the salad. Mary could only eat a few bites of breakfast. There were butterflies in her stomach again, and she was too excited to eat.

"Better eat a little more," Joe teased. "You'll need all the strength you can get. Next you'll faint when you stand before the bishop to be married."

"Just watch out that Arie doesn't trip over Dad's big feet," Mary shot back, good-naturedly.

Nancy giggled. She was wearing her new royal blue double-knit dress, and she also was too excited to eat. She stood at the window, watching for the first guests.

Finally everything was ready and in apple-pie order. The table waitresses, hostlers, and ushers were there, and the first guests began to arrive. The hostlers took care of the horses while the guests walked to the house. There they were greeted by ushers, who took their wraps. A few close friends brought wedding presents, which were unwrapped and displayed by gift receivers.

The bridal party was seated on chairs close to where the bishop and the ministers would stand while preaching. When the first hymn was announced, the ministers headed upstairs. Mary and Jacob followed them to the counsel room, where they were instructed in principles of Christian marriage—what Jacob's duties would be as a husband, and what Mary's duties would be as a wife.

When the counseling session was over, the wedding couple made their way downstairs and then through the narrow aisle made by guests seated on benches on either side. Mary was a beautiful and happy bride, but to look at her now, no one would guess her feelings. On her way back to her chair with bowed head and measured steps, she was as staid and demure as the most proper among them could wish. Jacob, also with bowed head, led her by the hand and looked fine and manly in his new plain-cut suit. They knew that all eyes were upon them.

Mary did not relax until the first minister began to preach. She felt less self-conscious then and listened carefully to the wedding sermon. Every word made a deep impression upon her. This time the instructions and advice about a Christian home and married life were for her and Jacob, and that fact made it especially meaningful. After a silent prayer, the bishop arose and expounded on the chosen passages in the Bible that portray home and life and harmonious living.

Jacob and Mary listened eagerly as with clarity he pointed out the beauty, holiness, and solemnity of marriage. Almost before they realized it, they were supposed to stand to be joined together in the bonds of holy matrimony.

The bishop arose and told the couple to step forward, then asked the age-old questions. Mary's voice trembled when she answered, and Jacob's was not much better. But it was valid, and the bishop clasped his hands over their joined right hands and pronounced the blessing.

After the services were over, Mary and Jacob went upstairs, waiting at the top of the steps to greet the line of well-wishers who would be coming when the singing was over.

"So now you're *Fraa* (Mrs.) Yoder," Jacob whispered adoringly, as he beheld his shining-eyed bride.

"Shhh!" Mary laid a finger on her lips. "They're coming."

When dinner was ready, the bridal party was seated at the corner table, adorned by the beautiful cake and other traditional dishes served at wedding feasts.

After all had eaten, the guests visited while the dishes were being washed. Then the afternoon was spent in singing hymns and visiting some more. Though the wedding dinner was formal and orderly, supper was much more casual. Instead of boys and girls sitting on opposite sides of the table, as they had at lunch, at suppertime each boy was supposed to choose a partner and sit with her, whether he wanted to or not.

Omar stood with the other sixteen-year-old boys, and when his turn came to choose a girl, he suddenly felt timid and bashful. What if the girl refused to go with him? As he walked up to the girls, Jacob's sixteen-year-old sister, Dorcas, gave him a bright smile. Gaining confidence, he held out his hand. She accepted and willingly went with him to the table. Omar felt a surge of gladness in his heart.

Ever since Deacon Gid's tobacco shed had burned down, he had harbored a secret fear that he would not be accepted by the Amish young folks. But Dorcas certainly was friendly, and he found his fears vanishing. She kept up a lively conversation during the meal, and Omar felt at ease with her.

Omar had never before noticed how pretty Dorcas was. She was sturdy, red-cheeked, and rosy, and when he compared her with Jewell, he marveled at the contrast. In comparison, Jewell was delicate, pale, and almost wan.

The rest of the evening was enjoyable for Omar. The young folks went to the barn to play various party games: there goes Topsy through the window, skip to my Lou, O-Hi-O, and six-handed reel. The barn floor had been swept yesterday for this very purpose, and lanterns were hung on the beams.

Omar found more healing for the ache in his heart since Jewell said her last good-bye. He felt accepted by this group of lively, friendly youngsters. Omar hoped they had forgotten all about the episode of the fire. Perhaps everything would turn out all right for him after all.

29

Charmed

THE wedding festivities were over, and the whole family pitched in to get everything put back in place. The benches were loaded into the church's gray bench wagon and hauled to the farm where the next church services were to be held.

One day just after the wedding, Joe was working in the shop. He tried out his scroll saw, thinking he could make a few Christmas presents for the younger ones. Mary came out of the house, a kerchief tied on her head.

"A letter for you," she called happily. "It must be from a girl, the way it's scented. Wow!"

Joe took the envelope. His heart skipped a beat when he saw the familiar handwriting. It was none other than Amelia's, flowery, cursive, and elegant. What was she up to now? Bursting with curiosity, he stuffed the letter into his pocket. He would wait until he was alone to open it.

Mary stayed to chat a while. But if she thought Joe would share the contents of the letter with her, she was disappointed.

"How did Arie enjoy being a guest of honor at the wedding?" Mary wondered. "Did it make her feel like one of the family?"

Joe shrugged his shoulders. "All right, I guess." He absentmindedly answered only her first question. His mind was on Amelia's letter.

Sensing that Joe was not in a talkative mood, Mary left for the house to make dinner. As soon as she left, Joe eagerly tore open the envelope with shaking hands.

Dear Joe,

Greetings of love. I'm writing to let you know that I'm sorry I ended our relationship and would be interested in resuming it again if you are willing. I guess you heard that Pete has gone back to Summerville, and that it's over between us. Please feel welcome to come back whenever it suits you. I feel badly about the way I treated you.

With love,
Amelia

Joe could hardly believe his eyes as he stood holding the note. Did Amelia really have the nerve to ask him to come back, all the while knowing he was going steady with Arie now? Something within him rebelled at the thought. Who did Amelia think she was, anyway?

But as the day wore on, Joe thought about it some more. Gradually that inward rebellion was turning to a spark of interest. What would it be like to keep company with Amelia again?

The old memories came flooding back. Amelia was easy and fun, while Arie was a girl of high standards. Amelia had quit him, but now he found his resentment against her melting away. As he thought of the dashing, fun-loving Amelia, his old feelings for her were again stirring within, warming his heart, as before. She was asking to be his again.

Joe felt helpless to resist her charms, her fascinating ways, her tinkling laugh. He knew he was slipping, but surely everything would turn out all right. Amelia would change after marriage and be willing to conform to the *Ordnung* a little better.

When Sunday evening came, Joe had made up his mind. He would tell Arie tonight that he wished to end their courtship.

As they drove home from the singing in the moonlight, Joe felt a deep sadness welling up within him. He had a deep respect for Arie. She was sweet and good, and he was fond of her. He cringed at the thought of hurting her. But the feelings he had for her were not as forceful, consuming, and intense as those he had for Amelia.

Chief had slowed to a walk. Should he tell her now, then just drop her off at her house, instead of going in? Or should he spend the evening there as usual, then tell her just before he left? Joe decided to tell her now. Clearing his throat, he started lamely, "Arie, I—I guess there's something I should tell you."

A feeling akin to panic welled up within him. How was he going to say it? He had never dreamed it would be so hard.

"Oh?" Arie responded in a low voice. "Is it bad news, Joe? You've been rather quiet all evening."

"Yes, ah—er—I don't know." Joe felt awkward as he fumbled for the right words. "I—I guess this is good-bye."

With a swift intake of breath, Arie looked at Joe. "You mean you don't wish to continue . . . that you won't be coming again?"

Joe nodded miserably in the darkness, but Arie knew the answer. They had arrived at Arie's place, and Chief drove to the hitching rack of his own accord.

There was a moment of stunned silence, then Arie said softly, "I guess I'll be going in then. Good-bye, Joe. God bless you!"

Then she was gone, walking swiftly to the house.

Suddenly Joe wanted to call her back, to tell her it was all a joke, and that he still wanted her. But she had already disappeared into the house. An overwhelming feeling of sadness and loss pressed down upon him, a sense that something good and beautiful was going out of his life forever.

Joe swallowed hard as he turned Chief around and headed out the lane. That feeling of desolation inside was threatening to choke him, and he blinked away the tears. Why had he broken off with Arie?

30

Character

THAT fall Omar began attending the Sunday evening singings and enjoying them, too. He was well accepted by the group and had made a lot of new friends. He found that he was thinking about Jewell less and less, and the hurt was fading away.

Mary and Jacob were busy with their postwedding visiting every weekend. During the winter months, the newlyweds made their rounds, staying with relatives and collecting presents from them. They were making plans for spring, when they

would move onto their farm in Summerville.

For a few months, Joe was Amelia's beau. Then one night on the way from singing, Joe was taking stock of their relationship. As usual, Amelia was talkative, but somehow her constant bright chatter failed to charm him anymore.

Joe found himself comparing her unfavorably with Arie on several counts. Amelia was self-centered and shallow; Arie had depth of character. Yes, Amelia had dainty, fascinating, and amusing ways; but Arie had a sacred influence on him. Her purity, goodness, and kindness had a bracing effect on him.

Suddenly and without a doubt, Joe knew that Arie was the one he loved and wanted. Amelia held no more fascination for him. If only he wouldn't have quit Arie! He suspected that Pete had tired of Amelia, too, and that was why he had gone back to Summerville.

When it was time for him to leave for home, Joe told Amelia he would not be coming back.

"*Fer was net* (why not)?" Amelia cried petulantly. "You can't do this to me, Joe. *Fer was?*"

"I—I don't really feel that we belong together," Joe tried to explain with compassion for her pain.

But Amelia wouldn't take no for an answer. "Please, Joe," she begged. "I'll do anything you say. I'll wear longer dresses and a larger head covering, if you want me to—anything."

Joe shook his head. "I—I've changed my mind

about coming back. It was a mistake. I'm sorry."

When Amelia found that Joe was firm in his decision, she resorted to tears. "You're the most heartless fellow I've ever seen," she called tearfully after him, as he stepped outside and gently closed the door.

Joe untied Chief and sank wearily unto the buggy seat. How had he ever gotten himself into such an awful mess? He mentally scolded himself for falling for Amelia the second time. If he wouldn't have, he could have spared himself the ordeal of quitting both Arie and Amelia.

"Dumm (stupid) Joe," he scolded himself. "How could you have been so *dumm?*" Suddenly a new thought struck him, and he sat bolt upright. What if Arie wouldn't take him back now? It made him feel sick at heart. He knew he didn't deserve her anymore, but, oh, how he wanted her. Yet he couldn't blame her the least bit if she refused him now.

As Joe drove homeward, he tried to figure out why he had made the mistake of resuming with Ameila, but there seemed to be no clear reason. He was feeling too badly to think straight.

He spent a sleepless night, tossing and turning. Would he be out of place if he drove over to Arie's place tomorrow? He simply had to talk to her. If only he could reach her by telephone! A letter would take much too long. Finally, just before dawn, Joe fell into a troubled sleep. It seemed like he had slept only a few minutes when Daed called him to begin choring. Wearily, he got out of bed.

By midmorning he could stand it no longer. He was tired, and the work didn't go well anyway. Joe simply had to find out how he stood with Arie. He hitched up Chief and drove to her home, through a biting wind that chilled him to the bone—but that was a minor problem. A light dusting of snow coated the ground.

What would Arie's folks think if he came to see her on a Monday morning, uninvited like this? He hoped they wouldn't assume he was unbalanced, but he knew his recent actions hadn't been fully rational.

Joe's heartbeat quickened when the Miller farm buildings came in sight. He drove to the tie railing, then stood undecided. Should he go to the kitchen door and knock? What if no one was home?

A moment later the door opened, and Arie came out the walk, a scarf tied on her head. Joe caught his breath. She had never before appeared so beautiful as she did now. He marveled at the sweet, fresh look on her face. Arie smiled in a sincere but slightly quiz-zical way, and her eyes were kind.

"Hello. Was it me you came to see?" she inquired, in that gentle, modulated voice of hers.

In a moment he was telling her the entire story, sparing no details, exposing his feelings and actions to the core. Arie listened quietly, the color rushing to her cheeks at times.

"I'm very, very sorry, Arie," Joe finished contritely. "*Kannscht vergewwe mich* (can you forgive me)? You are the one I love . . ."

After a long pause, half shyly he added, "May I start seeing you again?"

For a moment, Arie's heart fluttered queerly, and she lowered her gaze, unconsciously sweeping her cheeks with her lashes. Joe waited in trepidation for her answer. Would she perhaps want him to prove himself for awhile first? There was something about Arie that radiated wholesomeness, that made him want to be good and true for her sake.

Now her silence made him feel that, before asking, he should have waited, should have demonstrated more steady character. Why had he been so impatient? Yet he had felt that he couldn't stand the suspense, not knowing.

When Arie spoke, it was with sweet dignity and womanly grace. "You've made some rather quick decisions this last while, haven't you?"

Joe nodded. He had no excuses to offer. Besides, she was not accusing him; she was merely stating the facts.

She continued in a kind tone, "Would you be willing to wait several months? Then if you still want to, you are welcome to come back."

Joe's heart warmed within him, in spite of the cold, and a smile lit up his face. That was good enough for him.

"Thank you. That sounds reasonable to me," he softly agreed. "Well then, I should be going." He began to untie Chief's neck rope.

"Don't you want to come in and warm yourself before starting off?" Arie invited. "That wind sure is cold." Her kind eyes and sincere smile beckoned him.

Joe wavered for a moment, then answered, "If you would be alone, I would."

Arie smiled in that graceful manner of hers. "I understand," she said simply. "Thank you so much for coming, Joe. It has made me very happy."

"Your answer has made me very happy, too," Joe replied, his eyes shining. "Good-bye for now."

As he drove homeward, the healing oil of gladness surged through Joe's heart. He no longer minded the cold; he felt like singing and shouting for joy. Today he had been forgiven and accepted again. Arie sure had been kind and understanding.

Joe marveled at the invisible influence of sweetness and goodness that surrounded her, that made him want to do his best. Why had he been so blind to it before? Maybe because he had never compared her with Amelia before—the real Amelia, not the one he had glorified and mentally put on a pedestal.

He had learned a bitter lesson, but "all is well that ends well," he told himself. The future loomed bright and interesting before him.

_31_

Contentment

WINTER passed, and spring came once again to Whispering Brook Farm. Frogs were singing their evening songs, the birds joyously warbling and building nests, trees blossoming, and the air was lovely, scented by woods and earth and flowers.

Mary and Jacob were now settled on their farm in Summerville. Mom and Dad had promised Nancy that she could visit them for two weeks after the strawberry season was over.

It was Saturday forenoon, and Omar and Nancy

were mowing the lawn with the clattering hand-pushed reel mower. The grass was green and lush. Since it was too tiring for one person, they worked together, Omar pushing, and Nancy pulling, with baler twine around her waist and tied to the mower.

"I wonder if Daadi *hawwe net Heemweh* (isn't homesick) in heaven for all this," Nancy said impulsively, as they stopped to rest. She swept her arms wide at the loveliness of the fragrant, freshly mowed green grass, the sweet-scented white lilac bush, the blue sky, fresh breezes, and the bleeding heart bush in bloom. "Last spring he was still here to enjoy it, but now . . ." Her voice trailed off.

"Did you ever hear of the song, 'It's Always Springtime in Heaven'?" Omar asked.

Nancy wrinkled her brow. "I've heard heaven described as a celestial city, having streets paved with gold. I don't think I'd like to live in a city."

"Nobody really knows what heaven is like," Omar told her. "But I'm sure it's better and more beautiful than anything on earth. No one would wish to come back to earth, not even for spring-time."

Then Omar changed the subject. "Did you know that Daed might go to Nebraska to look at farms? He just told me this morning."

"Farms?" Nancy echoed blankly. "What for?"

"To move there, of course," Omar replied. "Land is getting awfully high priced around here. He has four boys to buy farms for, and if he sells this farm, he'll be able to buy at least three farms for the price of what this one would bring."

"Sell Whispering Brook Farm?" Nancy asked hollowly. *"Es kann yuscht net waahr sei* (it just can't be true)!"

"Well, it's not sure yet," Omar told her. "But three or four men are starting for Nebraska on Tuesday morning to look at land there, and Daed has a chance to go along. He sounded quite interested."

Nancy ran in to Mom. "Tell me it's not truc, Mamm," she begged. "Daed isn't going to sell our farm, is he?" Her eyes were wide with anguish.

Mom looked sympathetically at Nancy. "You think you wouldn't like that, don't you?" she asked tenderly.

Nancy shook her head, her eyes like brimming saucers.

"Maybe it wouldn't be as bad as you think," Mom went on, trying to think of something to say to comfort Nancy. "We'd still have each other. And who knows, maybe we'd have a nicer farm than this one."

Nancy turned and ran outside, tears blinding her eyes. She climbed to the haymow, flung herself face down on the bales, and wept bitterly. Never would she be able to leave dear Whispering Brook Farm. She loved every tree, every hill and dale, the lovely misty meadow, and best of all, she loved Whispering Brook.

Fresh sobs shook her body at the thought of

leaving it all. She might not be here next spring to see the hyacinths and daffodils and tulips come up, the lovely roses blooming on the arbor, the orchard in blossom, and the birds building their nests in her trees. There would be no more picnics in the orchard, no more toasting marshmallows over a bonfire by the brook, and no more climbing to her hideaway in the maple tree. Nancy hoped she would wake up to find that it was all a bad dream.

However, it was real. When Tuesday morning came, Dad was with the group that started for Nebraska. At night Nancy slept poorly. She could hardly bear the thought that someone else might sleep in her room and look at the lovely view of the farm from her window.

At mealtimes the food threatened to choke her. The idea of their lovely old-fashioned kitchen being theirs no longer! The familiar knotty pine cabinets, the wide window seat just right for curling up with a book, the built-in jelly cupboard where Nancy had a shelf of her own and kept her treasures—all would belong to someone else.

Tears were constantly near the surface during those trying days waiting until Daed came back. How could the boys be so heartless? They were actually *hoping* that Daed would sell their farm and buy land in Nebraska. Susie and Lydia were too little to care, so Nancy was alone in her despair.

On Monday a letter arrived saying the men would be home on Wednesday, but there was no clue in the letter as to whether or not they liked the farms in Nebraska.

On Wednesday afternoon Mom sent Nancy back to the spring for fresh watercress. They were hoping Dad would be home in time for supper, and watercress was one of his favorites. Nancy walked the half mile through the buttercup-filled meadow to the big tree where the spring flowed out of the ground and on down into Whispering Brook. Her tears flowed in imitation of the tiny stream.

It was all so dear and beautiful—the lush green meadow grass, and the new leaves on the trees. She waded into the spring with her boots on, carefully cut off the tender green cress, and filled her bag with it. This would make delicious watercress sandwiches.

As she headed for home, Nancy realized afresh how beautiful Whispering Brook Farm was, nestled there between the fir grove and the apple orchard. The homey sandstone house, the hay-filled barn where kittens played and the banties roosted, and the meadow with the brook flowing through it gave it a charm not matched by any other place Nancy had ever seen.

"Oh, I won't be able to leave it. I couldn't bear it," Nancy moaned again. Lassie was barking sharply when Nancy reached the yard. Who was that stranger coming up the road with a suitcase? A moment later Lassie recognized Dad, and her barks changed to tail wagging and yelps of welcome.

Steven and Henry raced out to meet him. "Daed, did you buy a farm?" they asked eagerly, in unison.

Their father laughed. "My, you're eager to find out." Joe and Omar had joined them, too, and they all followed Dad into the house. Mom and Grandma greeted him at the door.

"It's *so* good to be home." Dad thumped his suitcase on the floor and stretched out on the rocker. Lydia ran to him and tried to climb on his knee. He swung her up affectionately.

"Supper's almost ready." Mom's cheeks were pink and flushed from working over the cookstove. "Here, Nancy, you can make the salad." They were preparing Dad's favorite foods: roast chicken garnished with watercress, fresh hot rolls, mashed potatoes, sugar peas, new lettuce out of the hot bed, and shoofly pie.

Dad was telling about his trip, and the boys sat around him, listening spellbound. Nancy felt torn between wanting him to end the suspense by telling them whether or not they'd have to move, and wanting him not to say. As long as she didn't know, she could still hope.

"Supper's ready," Mom announced.

"Mmmm, all my favorites, and fresh meadow tea yet." Dad was grateful. "I sure missed your good cooking, Mamm."

The family bowed their heads to ask the blessing.

"I guess you're all wondering whether or not

we're moving to Nebraska," Dad began as he buttered a roll.

"Yes, please tell us," they all chorused.

"Well, I've decided not to buy land in Nebraska," Dad told them. "I never realized it was so far. We passed a lot of nice farms as we traveled through the states between here and Nebraska, and I decided it's not necessary to go so far. My wanderlust has been settled for awhile, but maybe sometime—maybe next year—I'll look at some farms a little closer to home."

"Well, so much for that," Joe responded simply.

Omar, Steven, and Henry looked crestfallen.

Nancy thought she would choke on her bite of roll. She was wildly, gloriously happy. All she heard was that they were not moving to Nebraska, not selling dear Whispering Brook Farm.

To her embarrassment, she found her eyes filling with tears. But they were tears of happiness, tears of joy. A feeling of peace and contentment filled her heart.

"*Danki, Gott* (thank you, God)," Nancy whispered as she hugged herself.

The Author

THE author's pen name is Carrie Bender. She is a member of an old order group. With her husband and children, she lives among the Amish in Lancaster County, Pennsylvania. Her books thus far are listed on page 2, above.

Bender is the popular author of the Whispering Brook Series, books about fun-loving Nancy Petersheim as she grows up surrounded by her close-knit Amish family, friends, and church community. This series is for children and a general audience.

The Miriam's Journal Series is also well appreciated by a wide reading public. These stories in journal form are about a middle-aged Amish woman who for the first time finds love leading to marriage. Miriam and Nate raise a lovely family and face life with faith and faithfulness. Bender portrays their ups and downs through the seasons, year after year.

The Dora's Diary Series tells about Miriam's adopted daughter, Dora, as she goes through her teen years, teaches school, has dates, and then is married and coping with a growing family.

Library Journal says, "Bender's writing is sheer poetry. It leads readers to ponder the intimate relationship of people and nature."

You may write to the author in care of Herald Press, 616 Walnut Avenue, Scottdale, PA 15683.